ARABIAN NIGHTS OF 1934

ALSO BY GEOFFREY O'BRIEN

PROSE

Hardboiled America
Dream Time: Chapters from the Sixties
The Phantom Empire
The Times Square Story
Bardic Deadlines: Reviewing Poetry, 1984-95
The Browser's Ecstasy
Castaways of the Image Planet
Sonata for Jukebox
The Fall of the House of Walworth
Stolen Glimpses, Captive Shadows: Writing on Film 2002-2012
Where Did Poetry Come From: Some Early Encounters

POETRY

A Book of Maps
The Hudson Mystery
Floating City: Selected Poems 1978-1995
A View of Buildings and Water
Red Sky Café
Early Autumn
In a Mist
The Blue Hill
Who Goes There

ARABIAN NIGHTS OF 1934

Geoffrey O'Brien

Terra Nova Press

NEWARK   CALLICOON   MATSALU

2023

© 2023 by Geoffrey O'Brien
ISBN: 978-1-949597-27-1

Library of Congress Control Number: 2023931792
All rights reserved.

published by:

Terra Nova Press
NEWARK   CALLICOON   MATSALU

Publisher: David Rothenberg
Editor-in-Chief: Evan Eisenberg
Proofreader: Tyran Grillo
Book design: Martin Pedanik
Set in Bell MT
Cover art: *Shadow Dance* by Martin Lewis,
reproduced by permission of the Estate of Martin Lewis.

printed by Tallinn Book Printers, Tallinn, Estonia

1 2 3 4 5 6 7 8 9 10

www.terranovapress.com

Distributed by the MIT Press, Cambridge, Massachusetts and London, England for Tom Robbins

What a blessing the talkies are! Lonely rooms to come home to in the evening after a day of loneliness no matter if we work with hundreds and come in contact with thousands. Lonely dinners, lonely walks, and lonely nights! Now, overnight it seems, our friends have multiplied fourfold.

Letter to the editor,
Motion Picture Classic, 1930

Without your love
It's a honky tonk parade
Without your love
It's a melody played in a penny arcade

"It's Only a Paper Moon" (1933)
Lyrics by E. Y. Harburg and
Billy Rose, music by Harold Arlen

Dorothy at 17

Arabian Nights of 1934

This Modern Age

(1) it is all brand new this morning

(2) you have to be fast

(3) lunch break

(4) the city is a modern laboratory

(5) the machine is noisy

(6) trained to play a decisive role

(7) it all has to do with invisible rays

City Streets

(8) the world is starting to wiggle

(9) talking is fighting

(10) her eyes move over the surface of things

(11) corner carved out for refuge

(12) the city is shaped like your body

(13) cornet solo in smoke

(14) emergency ward

(15) a grid of dread

(16) peculiar hobbies

Loose Ankles

(17) the keyhole brigade

(18) problems of modern marriage

(19) the woman who considered herself
cosmopolitan

(20) homebodies without a home

(21) up against head winds

(22) world without rules

(23) a certain amount of shattered glass

Fast Life

(24) weird wrong turns

(25) it takes longer to tell than to happen

(26) box factory

(27) he never even found out

(28) a lot of slick talk

(29) the only thing that matters

(30) too slow on the uptake

(31) everybody knows everybody

(32) no money in the jungle

Blood Money

(33) stake out an empty lot

(34) not a trace of you lingers

(35) silent glares

(36) it is always some gimmick

(37) black cars tear zigzags

(38) the world is in your pocket

(39) it wasn't even his gun

(40) those last two seconds

Doorway to Hell

(41) into the back country

(42) streets made of stares

(43) behind a wall of mountains

(44) a cherished poison

(45) a mystery

(46) palm trees in shifting light

(47) along the edges of the uncharted world

Turn Back the Clock

(48) an erratic crackling sound

(49) calendar pages flipping

(50) guilty curiosity

(51) nothing but air and rock

The Crash

(52) something died inside

(53) like knocking back a stiff one

(54) petal upon petal floated down

(55) the final cocktail frolic

(56) the only man who could save everybody

(57) finding out what it is like

(58) industrialized hells

(59) the eyes of broken men

(60) sticking it to the bellyachers

Laughing Sinners

(61) very exclusive premises

(62) silk crepe contours

(63) old coots can't really win

(64) finely sliced baloney

(65) they can't get arrested

Bright Lights

(66) the guy that made Broadway famous

(67) the mouse not the message picture

(68) the blank verse of the twentieth century

(69) steal it from somebody else's dream

(70) every last bit of chitchat and backtalk

(71) the bait

The Code

(72) do the movies give them ideas

(73) to be warriors

(74) one picture one plotline one audience

After Tomorrow

(75) people I met in a dream

(76) how much they could leave out

Aloysius at 18

Dorothy After the Show

Some Pre-Code Movies

DOROTHY AT 17

From far below a vibrating rumble comes and a door bursts open. A woman in a star-spangled robe steps through the gap. She is the woman from the picture in *The Arabian Nights.* The rumble comes again. By now I'm completely awake. It's Mine No. 7, seven blasts around daybreak. I fall back into sleep until the car horns start up on East Main. All through the day I can tell time by noises, the mine signals and noon whistles and alarms at rail crossings. At night by night trains and fog horns on the river. I've always been hearing them. Waking for the second time I remember what day it is, my day to be free.

It worked out so nicely by accident, the little ones going to stay overnight with Aunt Sue yesterday, and Mother and Daddy driving to Scranton this morning for the memorial service of Mister Bednar who died last Tuesday. And Mother finally having to admit I'm old enough to look after myself. By the time I get downstairs they're already heading out the door, Mother telling me to make sure to have my key when I go out and a bunch of other things she thinks I'm incapable of remembering. She can hardly believe that anyone but her knows what they are doing. What pleasure to have everything to myself, my own breakfast of toast and jam and cocoa with no one talking at me, straightening up the kitchen so no one would even know I'd been there, and then my room for a last look at *The Arabian Nights*—the colors of the illustrations are so bright and strange I could stare at them forever—but it has to go back to the library. That will be my first stop, my only plan. Except the movies.

I move along the frayed hall carpet where my feet
follow always the same pattern, then down the front
stoop and into the day. Almost trembling to have hours
unaccounted for. Free to do nothing or what other
people call nothing. To look and breathe and walk.
There is an angle and distance from which everything
looks full of promise, as if it couldn't wait for you. I
follow the path I invented through streets whose every
surface and texture I know too well even to think
of it as "seeing." I'm wrapped inside it. How many
times, awake with eyes shut, waiting for sleep or for
the night to end, have I counted the wooden steps of
the front stoop and traced in my head the zigzag path
to Market Street. I dart through shortcuts perfected
long ago, counting off shop windows, hardware,
footwear, smocks, frocks. Every crack in every curb.
The flaking paint on signs. The slightest change in
coloring or pattern jumps out. Something moved. A
dog crossed the street. Someone on the second floor
slid a curtain open a few inches. The mystery of what
could be going on in that room. Who is hiding there,
from what, for how many years. Otherwise the whole
town would fall back into itself until it wasn't there. A
flat faded surface like the painted backdrops they haul
out for school plays. A dull weight like a permanent
low-grade headache. Am I already where I will end up
being, without knowing it? Nobody tells you where
you are until you have already been there for a long
time. The place is there before the name. You don't
know where it is on a map. You don't know what a
map is. You may not know where you were until years
later you find yourself somewhere else. Am I already

what I will end up being? An actress playing the part
of a child. The same as in the silly pageant when I
played a queen. How could anyone tell? Who could
ever know what I think, or what I see? It is private to
me, mine not theirs, not anyone's. What happened in
books in the past, the Indian massacre and the battle at
the fort, is like a dream but it happened. It could have
happened anywhere. I could be anywhere. But this
is where all these people came. There were mills and
mines and railroads, houses for sale in the mountain
towns, streets for shopkeepers. At dinner people talk
about where they came from and how they ended up
here. Mother and her sister start talking in Hungarian
when they don't want the rest of us to hear. And once
they got here it seems everything came to a halt. The
story was over except for work which never ends for
anybody.

When I walk alone I make up my own story, I become
it. I move across the trolley tracks and quickly through
an alley cluttered with cast-away machine parts, past
the old elementary school abandoned now because
it's sinking slowly into the ground, the coal mining
weakened the soil they say, and finally into the library
where I spend hours, but not today because I don't
want the whole day to get eaten up by books. I hand
The Arabian Nights to Mrs. Cowell and head downtown
toward People's Shoe Store and the Pontiac dealership
and Leventhal's, the loan company and the five and
dime, the white marble banks and post offices that
will always feel like stone palaces. A banner over the
entrance of the fire station. The department store

where you put your dollar in a tray and it travels by
conveyor belt to the cashier on the next floor and then
your change comes back in the same tray. Notions
counter a jumble of pins and thimbles. Electric fans.
Wool bathing suits. In the window of the piano
parlor the sheet music fresh from the packing boxes.
Pastel pictures of flower gardens and evening bowers
decorated with colored fabrics of Arabia. Silk gowns
cut and trimmed like precious glass sculpture. Sunsets
over red seas. I walk among the women in the hat shop.
Every sound they make is familiar, every hesitation
and chuckle and sigh. A music of saying nothing new.
The place is voices. Here in English, on other streets
in Hungarian or Polish or Czech or Welsh. Talking
about the others in languages they don't understand.
The Czechs think they're better than the Hungarians,
the Hungarians think they're better than the Poles, and
the native-born Americans think they're better than
anyone even if they don't say it out loud. If they could
hear themselves. The way they go on saying the same
things again and again. You have to laugh.

Out on the street the outlines of the objects seem
sharper today. They stand out in the sun. Even railings
and paving stones are waking up. Once upon a time
I was invisible and almost didn't have a body. Secret
histories never to be told. I could stare as long as I
liked at a trapped wasp buzzing between the window
and the screen or the smoke curling from a neighbor's
chimney. I could let my eyes travel over my bedspread
until only by looking I knew the texture of every
separate strand of fiber it was woven of, like a hidden

country. Like no other surface anywhere. Nothing—the
nicks on the handle of the rolling pin in the kitchen
drawer or the smeared cigar ash in Daddy's ashtray
or the smell of day-old soup reheated on a morning
last winter after I was sick—was like anything else
anywhere. Apple blossoms that fell in the back yard
after a wind gust I don't know how many years ago.
The silence in the school auditorium when I stayed
on after everybody else went home. Nothing repeats.
The tiny differences are chiseled into the surface of
things like the mark someone would make on a wall
to keep track of time. A condemned person who had
no calendar, the Man in the Iron Mask or the Prisoner
of Chillon. The sounds and edges became part of
me before I had a chance to decide if that was what I
wanted. I looked at a raindrop sliding down a window
pane and felt I could be that raindrop. What a destiny,
to be a globule of water pressed on glass and moving
downward unavoidably toward the cracked gray
paint coating the window sill. What a collision, like
passengers on the Titanic going down, far from any
rescue boat. How terrible to drown. What a word is
fate. What a thing to be born, wrapped in a whirling
web and no getting out of it except by not being.
Jump off the wheel. Why would I want to. I of all
people. Who have never been given a task I could not
accomplish. Who can cook a meal, keep a house in
order, take care of my little brother and sister when
Mother and Daddy are both working. As they mostly
do since the times got bad, she in her beauty shop and
he in the mine office, where it kills him to spend his
days instead of playing music. I get an A on every

test in Latin. Gallia est omnis divisa in partes tres.
Am tops at volleyball and swimming. Have organized
campsites and found paths on mountains by use of
compass. But these were tasks done for others. What
I cannot say is like the Shelley ode we read in class.
Wild spirit moving everywhere. Reciting lines by
Shakespeare I was a channel. At some moments even
my own name is new, the name of someone I never
knew I was. Transformed, the way in *The Arabian
Nights* the population of the city became a bay full of
multicolored fish, the prince was turned half to stone
and could not rise from his throne, the old man of the
sea changed shape from one second to the next. Or in
the book of Greek myths the way bodies become birds
or statues or trees or streams of water. Forms melt at
the touch of a god. Her hair was changed to leaves, her
arms to branches. The words contain turmoil, the same
way spring flowers seem violent. What a thing if the
invisible gods were real. As real as music. After how
many thousands of days the world changed. Never to
be found again as it was. Has this just happened. Or
does it happen over and over and I forget.

There is no way to write this down but it is all over
the place. On the radio Bing Crosby has the world
on a string and all at once for no reason I do too.
Everything hangs on one string. And I'm almost where
I was heading all along, trying not to be too impatient
to get a first look at the posters of coming attractions
outside the movie theater. Going to the pictures where
everything I see inside will be new. Coming around the
corner within sight of the faces and lettering never

quite imaginable until they are in front of you. Movies
that have come and gone, movies that are yet to come.
The words burst out and make a noise in the head.
BORN TO BE BAD. Was Loretta Young born to be
bad, and how and why? ALL MEN ARE ENEMIES.
Is it true? A woman in a long dark gown stares out,
angry and arms akimbo. THE LOST PATROL. The
one my brother loved, that he played in the back
yard with his school friends, where all the men are
trapped in a desert oasis and shot down one by one by
unseen Arabs. WEST OF THE DIVIDE. A cowboy
on a white horse. BEAST OF BORNEO. Never. A
monstrous ape. The weirdest triangle ever filmed. I
don't want to look at that one. But today's feature is
what I wanted to see. PARIS INTERLUDE. Come to
the Left Bank of gay Paree and leave your troubles
behind. The daring Art Students' Ball. Gorgeous
fashion. Feel your pulse pound faster. Heartbreak and
sudden romance. Madge Evans who is almost as pretty
as Ann Dvorak. I approach the glass booth, slide the
coins under the slot, take the ticket and grasp it for
fear of losing or dropping it.

Once the lights go down inside everything will be a
surprise. Even something that looks familiar is a kind
of surprise, like seeing my own home, my own town,
from the outside for the first time. Mirror images of
foldable Formica card tables and soda fountains. A
car at a filling station, handsome young boy pumping
gas. Bandstands in the park where people stroll on
July afternoons. Mill workers going home. A sign
outside a camp meeting in the woods—HEAVEN OR

HELL?—that makes me think of Bible School last
summer where I got a pin for attendance. A girl on the
screen who might be me, the way I imagined a year
ago I would look someday, getting ready for a prom. In
the dark everything starts to slide apart. The screen
is like a membrane. It lines up with my world along
the edges and with a click it blurs in the middle and
a passageway opens into another space. Like Alice's
looking-glass. I don't know where I'm going. Into
what future world. I have not yet known fever jungles
or narcotic fiends. Or wives who carry on with other
women's husbands. Who knows what goes on among
the roughest of the mineworkers. People I was told to
keep a distance from. You don't know how thin the line
is until you cross it. I never saw a gangster that I knew
of. Nobody ever yet said "get wise to yourself sister"
in that rasping tone that now is a voice I can tune into
in my head. Or mimic almost exactly if I choose. The
sandpaper tone of some traveling salesman or racket
boss. So many voices. Some stammer out of pitiful
shyness, some roar to prove how loud they can laugh,
some tease in a naughty playful way, or sometimes not
so playful, some go to pieces from feeling more than
they can stand. In the dark, in the beginning, it's better
to clear all that out. Start blank. If you really want to
watch you have to surrender from the start. Don't be
distracted by thoughts. But just when the surrender
is complete, when it's too late, I remember that bad
things can happen in this dark. It has happened before.
They took me to see the Phantom and afterward I
wished I could have closed my eyes and never seen
that face. How many years it took to rub it out. Not

rub it out even, I know perfectly well it is there under the layers I piled on it. How long it took to learn, at first by failing again and again and finding myself frightened beyond any reason, not to go near the place inside me where he is hidden. A person can be lured into a terrible place. It has been the fate of lost girls and innocent children. There is only one terrible place. Sometimes it looks like a cage crawling with snakes, sometimes like an underground corridor stalked by a hooded intruder, sometimes an alley where a child loses her way and will never be allowed to go home. Erased as if she never had been. I don't want to be dragged back into my own shadow. This is what it is to be nowhere at all and not able to get out. Daddy's sister tried to kill Mother with a knife. They took her to a hospital with great stone walls where she was never allowed to walk outside again. I was taken to see her in her room there and that became another hidden face.

Things happen that don't fit into the world. Nothing is more upsetting than what occurs in the most ordinary places, the places where those who live there say that nothing ever happens. In schoolyards or attics or garages, in the middle of town at odd hours, little acts of cruelty and craziness are taking place all the time. Boys torment kittens in barns. They will spoil the world if you let them. The tiniest unexpected meanness makes the sky heavy. The look of someone who somehow doesn't want you to be there. There is an embarrassment in being hurt. A disappointment suspended where no one can reach. Leave it behind.

The movie is beginning. I am elsewhere, I am empty, I am myself. The other world begins here and glides toward distant glimmering cities. Unimaginable outposts, dark wharves, dim glow of lamps in Chinatown alleys, the tinkling of bells at dusk. Vast packed music halls. The images of things imported from far away by rails, by gangplanks, airships, systems of pulleys, cunning strands of cable. A murmuring from across oceans of French accordion songs, bearded Russian philosophers, Spanish dancers in black lace with castanets. And the wild places beyond any city, armed encampments, appalling wonders of glaciers and limestone caverns. Are they looking at these scenes in such places? Do the inhabitants of the rubber plantations and prospectors' camps look up and see their world on the screen? Do fallen women and gangsters watch movies of fallen women and gangsters, do bankers and countesses see themselves reflected? Everybody can see everything in the dark.

I am already thinking about how it will be to get on the train and go away from where I am, carried toward one of the cities. After the movie ends I want it to be the future already. Candle-lit dinners are taking place in Manhattan apartments adorned by strange masks and glistening tapestries. The guests know what is rarest and most beautiful in the world. So witty and self-assured they are. You would never feel embarrassed for any of them. In this enclave elegant women, sensitive and sharp-eyed, speak in low tones, alert to every possible danger. One of these women moves past the lacquered Chinese screen toward the

balcony, a drink in her hand. A figure of pure elegance
like Ann Dvorak. I have already begun to be her. The
man at her side is whispering something charming
to her as they stand by the open window looking
out at a moonlit suspension bridge. This will really
happen. In the world of the future, cleverer things will
be said than even Robert Montgomery or Adolphe
Menjou ever managed. Words will be written finer
than Shaw or Maugham. I can feel myself already
part of that brilliant troupe. Free to make a bright
gossamer remark that holds the table's attention for a
moment or to dissolve with my chums into giggles, like
schoolgirls again, at home where we are meant to be in
the city from which we can never be expelled. Where
I will arrive when I am done with being here in the
meantime, waiting for everything to start. And all the
other kids, where will they go. If they go anywhere.
The town will move to the same rhythm as always,
the tavern noisy with vulgar hunters bragging about
their kills, the same outbursts of laughing on picnic
days and the same rounds of songs toward sunset, row
row row your boat, the same smells from the coal bins,
the same horrible flypaper dangling at the back of
the hardware store because they never change it often
enough, saving money I guess…

ARABIAN
NIGHTS
OF 1934

This Modern Age

it is all brand new this morning

The sun rises in the middle of the field. The newspapers call this the dawn of the age of aeronautics. There is nothing like going up first thing in the brisk American morning. This young man is happy to be alone for the moment, with the sky to himself. The constant engine roar is home to him. A beat-up biplane left over from the war but a nice little baby, handles pretty good. When the clouds part he sees the city spread out. Shiny like a freshly mopped linoleum floor. The iron works and the commercial buildings look like wooden blocks straight from the Sears Roebuck catalogue. He checks off the layout as he flies over: the bridge, the gas plant, the depot, the five and dime, the movie palace, the park where he can almost make out the band box and the Civil War cannon. People on the street hear the buzz and look up. Three office girls stroll to work with a bounce that makes them look glad to be headed there. They imagine they can see the pilot leaning out and waving to them. He gets a jolt out of swooping so low it practically knocks their hats off. Across miles of space they face each other like living models for the posters of coming attractions outside the Rialto. SUNNY SKIES. CHEER UP AND SMILE. THE AGE FOR LOVE. It is all brand new this morning. Even the sky seems freshly invented. *Young and healthy*, full of bounce and ready for all chances. They feel like stepping out. There are songs about feeling this way. Songs about smiles, about the street, about the sun.

you have to be fast

Everything became modern and is about to start for the first time. The sky won't stay empty for long, not in this day and age. To the aerodrome five miles beyond the town limits comes a couple speeding along the turnpike in a roadster. Really stepping on it. They can't wait to be alone together, he in his camel's hair overcoat, she with a floral hat from Bon-Ton. They go up in a new model—cute little two-seater. It is her first time. Once they hit the right altitude they flirt with winks. Deafened by engine noise and loving it. Like misbehaving schoolkids they pass scribbled notes back and forth. Back at the hangar, a rawboned young engineer is feverishly jotting down formulas on a scratchpad as he zeroes in on the specs for his new invention. *It isn't a pipe dream. It's the greatest motor in the world.* His best buddy—even if they do have eyes for the same girl—is too preoccupied to pay much attention as he dreams about taking over the South American mail route. Gulps his black coffee and scrams off to the tarmac. Never saw his feet touch the ground. You have to be fast if you want a shot. *Watch my dust.*

lunch break

In the magic city that airplanes fly over the three office girls sit around in the diner on their lunch break. Always with one eye on the clock. Except maybe for the reckless blonde in the polka dot dress who is always going on dates with men she hardly knows. She gets by on sheer nerve. Even if her pal—the one who wears glasses and stays late at the office while the other slips out for a rendezvous with the new beau—feels like she has to do her worrying for her. Though for the life of her she doesn't know why she should care, considering. Still and all they are great chums. Never mind about not paying back that loan last Friday. Or borrowing her nicest hat without asking. *You never wear it anyway.* And then there is the new hire, fresh out of a convent or something. Demure, you might call her, or just agonizingly bashful. Doesn't know any slang and honestly believes they will be in terrible trouble if they get back late to the office. Her pal needs to clue her in: *Don't worry about Mr. Cartwright, I know just how to handle him.* With a broad wink as she chews her gum. Some people get away with anything. It's the same situation always. There's one who knows and doesn't care, one who cares but doesn't know, and then the one who knows and cares and sits up alone at three a.m. wondering where it ever got her. Her tart little side remarks go right over the heads of her lunchmates. No telling where any of this might be leading. Or who might come around the next corner, pull up to the curb on any excuse and strike up a line of chat. Anyway they can dream.

the city is a modern laboratory

As you descend through the clouds toward the city the details come into focus. You're inside the hive: the barber singing La donna è mobile as he presses a hot towel around the neck of a freshly shaved customer—the schoolteacher wiping off Latin conjugations with a chalk eraser while her students steal a glance out the window at the sound of the plane's buzz—the barkeep slicing foam off a stein of beer—the near-sighted linotype operator setting a headline about the municipal bond proposal—the bank teller peering through barred windows at the restless customer drumming his fingers on the counter to make it clear he doesn't have all day—the heavyset red-nosed cop directing intersection traffic—the perpetually nerve-wracked radio announcer stepping up to the microphone clutching ad copy for the antacid spot—the young wife in flower-patterned apron daydreaming as she slides her roast into the oven—the painter stepping back to study his model by the sunshine that pours in through the skylight, accenting her cheekbones the way he intends to immortalize them on canvas—the organ grinder on the corner with his monkey and the band of wide-eyed street urchins clustering around. The city is a modern laboratory. Doctors and engineers planned it. Trucks deliver its foodstuffs. Jagged edges become obsolete. All its parts—ramps, tracks, tubes, wires, cables, channels, funnels, gutters—are designed for interconnection. It all fits: a miracle of our time. White wheeled rectangles slide through snug portals. Cylinders move along runways by pneumatic pressure. Plates meet plates and mesh. The surfaces are so smooth and the rims so rounded you want to run your fingers over them. Every detail is as welcoming as fresh-baked rolls laid out behind streak-free windows. New species of plastic model the outlines of a future without rust. The shapes of the city flow out like milk into a streamlined glass bottle.

the machine is noisy

This is the most complex piece of equipment ever designed. On top of that you can live inside it. Every possible way that wheeled contraptions can zigzag around in midtown was foreseen on some drawing board. Stuff people do day in day out without thinking—draw the blinds, step off the curb into a touring car, pay the bus driver, enter and exit through noiseless revolving doors—geniuses planned that! You could get the shakes just thinking about so much precision. If you didn't know it might look like chaos when folks out on the street get tangled in car traffic, foot traffic, women with oversized hat boxes clambering into taxis, men waving cigars, dogs tugging frantically at their leashes, messenger boys darting through openings in the crowd, alarms shrieking, office elevators landing with a thud. The machine is noisy. Press a button and the gears revolve. There is a jolt of barks and rumbles and industrial whistles. Conveyor belts kick into action. Nozzles spray liquid into infinite rows of identical vats. El trains rattle overhead. Propellers spin until the sky is blotted out by bone-shaking roars. Announcements scream from loudspeakers that can hardly handle the volume. Cars backfire. Horns honk continuously. Drivers yell from taxi to taxi in half a dozen languages. Mobs of workers stream toward the employees' entrance, to be swallowed up in the clatter of a thousand typewriters. Eight hours later, mobs of partygoers spread out from the business district toward every pleasure spot marked out by sinuous neon figures flashing on and off: a dancing girl, a trumpeter tilting his horn, a stream of liquid pouring into a martini glass. After a hard day they relax by shouting. Out of a window comes hot radio music. In alleyways the children yell and bang on tin cans with sticks as loud as they are able.

trained to play a decisive role

The blueprint of the new city is so elegant you could hang it on a wall. A masterpiece of modernist design for the highbrows, for the students in lab coats a specimen of engineering to be marveled at. They went to college to learn to be sharp enough for the approval of their German-born instructor. They let off steam with childish pranks. Hide around the corner—barely stifling their giggles—and wait for the firecracker to explode under the podium, then scamper before the old man catches sight of them. He is on to their antics, anyway, and that is all perfectly correct, *the normal expression of healthy animal instincts.* For all his intimidating scowl and beard there is an occasional appreciative gleam in his eye. *In these halls, gentlemen, a new generation of Americans is being trained to play a decisive role in the world.* When they come home between terms, the folks can barely understand a word they say anymore. Medical students have no further use for superstitions and home remedies. Nowadays it is all about vaccines and pasteurization and the Lord knows what else. It's a tough curriculum they've chosen. Some of them are going to wash out. The one who drinks too much from the flask in his back pocket and then sleeps through crucial lectures on the symptoms of peritonitis and botulism—that one, you can bet on it, will never amount to anything. He'll sell his services to criminal gangs and get summoned after midnight to tend a bullet wound by bare bulb light in a run-down hotel room, his hand shaking as he struggles not to botch the incision. Meanwhile his roommate—a steadier sort, ambitious but not arrogant—will pass the exams, grow a discreet moustache, and one day find himself on an ocean liner bound for Vienna. Vienna? Can it really be possible? *You listen to me, my boy, you're not going to Vienna to drink beer and listen to waltzes.* After years of self-denial he will emerge from the lab with a cure for the pestilence ravaging Central America. By the time his hair turns white they will have chiseled his name above the entrance to the new wing.

it all has to do with invisible rays

Pictures come to life. Colors were never so bright before. In cavernous gymnasiums the harmonies of an invisible orchestra are piped in by wire. Flying automobiles cruise aerial boulevards. Stacked one on another in crystalline towers, the breeze-swept apartments are splendid with floral displays delivered fresh from outlying archipelagoes. In the cloud city the doors open at the touch of a button and hot meals glide on transoms. No need for cooks or waiters in the new world. Thoughts become actions. With miracle fabrics torn clothes mend themselves. The movie palace is the oracle of the approaching change. Motionless in your seat you watch what will be arriving next week or next decade, unless it is already happening somewhere in secret. Science is magic. Or was magic always really science. One way or another it all has to do with invisible rays. The most arcane powers rely on technical secrets soon to be laid bare. Almost anything is possible, if a psychic crook can read a safe's combination from a bank manager's mind, even if he has to strain a little to get the numbers right—pausing in mid-turn while the police inspector looks at him suspiciously. Or if, through hypnosis, a man can be induced to fire a weapon at a complete stranger, in obedience to the will of someone miles away. These are proven powers, yet not so different from the legendary capacity of certain Gypsy women to read a baby's future from a birthmark. It was always science except the scientists hadn't figured it out yet. And they still haven't! The deepest lore remains unfathomed. It is too easy for us modern sophisticates to dismiss what the ancient ones understood so well. The curse set in motion by the opening of King Tut's tomb— that cascade of multiple inexplicable deaths striking down all who violated the sanctity of his resting place—was nothing but the application of age-old knowledge buried beneath the sands. In the shadow of the pyramids men achieved refinements of electromagnetism and atomic affinity about which we can only speculate. Some future genius will recover this lost wisdom for our benefit. If somebody else doesn't get there first and pervert it for his own twisted intentions. He may well already be at work among us. It is almost a certainty. The crooks who work for him know him only as Mr. X. They have never seen his face. Hotel chambermaids and cab drivers and the administrators of private clinics are bound to him by an unholy allegiance. From phone booth to phone booth the alerts are relayed. When a federal agent is about to reveal who Mr. X really is, just as his lips are forming the first syllable of the name, a bullet shatters the window. The tinkle of broken glass is followed by footsteps running down the fire escape. The secret has once more gone missing in alleys with no lights.

City Streets

the world is starting to wiggle

By day in the city every minute is a parade. And the nights aren't bad either if you don't mind taking your chances. What a kick in the head to see the whole works laid out clean and sleek and for free. *It's the greatest town in the world and don't let anybody kid you.* Each body stands out trim like a stage actor or a mannequin in a shop window. A catalogue of poses as good as the Follies. The fluent curves of Bakelite figurines behind glass. No more clutter, nothing bulky or shapeless. Every item on display has got plenty of air around it. Like posters showing off the newest line in everything from wristwatches to bedroom slippers. You get the urge to move the way the objects are shaped. Put some pep into it. The world is starting to wiggle to a new and snappy cadence. There is a knack to every little thing, the way a hat should fit on a head, the sound that shoes should make on a dance floor, the tempo for taking a car around a sharp bend. It's an art form just navigating through all this stuff. A syncopated fusion of art forms. This is how to walk through a door. This is how to hail a cab. This is the way to hit the street at five when the office slaves are throwing off their chains and streaming from the elevators into the glittering lobby. And then after a jazzy sequence of raps on the door Johnny the Kid steps into his girlfriend's cold water flat doing a soft shoe routine, launching into a song: *Life is just a bowl of cherries.* What a wink he gives her. The gall of the man. Pure nerve. But like music. Even a gangster's biography is a dance number, a dance number ending in death.

talking is fighting

City people inhabit canyons and scrounge to get the best view. LOVE FOR BREAKFAST. DO YOU INHALE? IS MARRIAGE A MENACE TO ROMANCE? WHY CAN'T MOVIE STARS STAY IN LOVE? DOUBLE YOUR WEEKEND FUN WITH A KODAK. SPEARMINT STEADIES THE NERVES. Slogans look down like the gods of the mountain over humming sidewalks and aisles and side streets jammed with people who talk fast all day long and into the night. You'd have to write it all down in a notebook to keep track, but who could write that fast. Watch that guy moving like a rocket. Not a dime in his pocket but he sure has plenty of talk. – *You look familiar. – I'd like to be.* In the city you will be knocked out of the box if you can't keep it coming. *You're about the niftiest trick I ever saw, why don't we give it a whirl?* Footloose guys on Saturday night want to let the world know they are there. – *Take a gander at that one. – Did you say a gander? I wonder how she'd go for a goose.* Giving every girl the eye until they get called out for it. *Take a good look. It's free.* Talking is fighting. All the time it is nothing but slickers against yokels, roughnecks against prudes, wiseguys against greenhorns, girls from finishing school against barflies from the school of hard knocks, effete art dealers against hard-case mobsters, high hats against panhandlers. Not one ever stops cranking it out— *try this on for size, more laughs than a barrel of monkeys*—the spiel of a traveling salesman, the come-on of a strung-out carny hand, the intricate hard luck story of a con man preparing to nail his mark, the dirty jokes of drunken conventioneers. *Say you oughta be in pictures with a line like that.* If he wanted to, that washed-up old-timer with the gift of gab could take a long slug of his rotgut rye and summon up everything he ever eavesdropped on, play it back like a phonograph, the pep talks of football coaches, the harangues of prison wardens and drill sergeants, the barroom poetry recitals of well-educated soaks, the back-street gallantries of burnt-out ladies' men, the back-street comebacks of women too wise to fall for them. *Save that gag for the tourists. I came to be paid, not pawed. You do all your talkin' with your hands.*

her eyes move over the surface of things

Barely out of her teens, if that, she slips alone into the middle of the noise. The quiet one. The serious one. It isn't the noise she craves. But she must pass through it to get to the other side of it. She wants to be somewhere else, away from what has always surrounded her. Stand solitary on a high terrace in the sun, or in a shaded alcove blocked off by lacquered screens or French-style folding doors. High above—separated out—or deep inside where the rest of the mess can't get at her. She still has not gotten used to what she's been hearing and seeing all her life. Something dies inside her at the idea that another day is beginning. It will be exactly the same as the ones that went before. She keeps this thought to herself because none of those lugs would understand. Or the women either. She is angry. She is sorry for her father. She hates her father because he has become one of them, unable to listen or see. She hates her mother for never letting up on him and driving him to drink in the first place. She is sensitive and discontented. She wants to lean over the railing on a ferryboat watching the pattern its wake makes. If there is nowhere else there is the rooftop. Even in the most ragged neighborhoods no one can take away the stars. She is still entranced by the first poem she ever read, a sonnet in a book a teacher gave her as a graduation gift. She has never knowingly told a lie up until now. Or maybe everything she ever said was a lie. How could she tell anybody? Her only truth is her silence. Her eyes move over the surface of things—the rusted radiator, the floral wallpaper drained of color, the broken toy truck abandoned on the stoop, the closed shutters of the room where she can almost hear the sickly child struggling to breathe, the haggard face of the jealous milkman's beaten-down wife across the way—as if seeing it all for the first time.

corner carved out for refuge

To be modern is to have the right to be alone. To exist at all, for a few precious uninterrupted moments, is to be alone. You could be alone watering a plant. You could be alone with a book open on your lap and managing not to take in a single word. *Just daydreaming, I guess.* The great struggle of life comes down to nothing more than a rented space. No matter how tiny, as long as you can lock the door behind you. Your own soundproofed interior. With drapes. The walls decorated with images of ancient fountains. How about a uniformed doorman? A waiter wheels in a tray with platters of delicacies and champagne in an ice bucket. Your companion—this man you hardly know but feel you have known forever—makes you laugh in spite of yourself. With him certainly you are no longer alone. He is the concert pianist who picked you out of the crowd for the intensity of your gaze during the Rachmaninoff. The sincerity of your reaction was instantly apparent to him. One tableau melts into another, like a concerto. A roguish guardsman catches sight of you hanging laundry on a line in a courtyard—he on horseback, in the shadow of the chateau's ramparts— while the other peasant girls join arms and sing, one smile giving way to another as in a daisy chain. For a moment a shared glance blots out everything. The picture dissolves into the metal boundaries of a fire escape. The cage's edge, the smallest corner carved out for refuge.

the city is shaped like your body

To be modern is never to be alone. You are in a car—your friends are in a car—weaving deliriously past midtown marquees. DESERT NIGHTS. THE MIDNIGHT KISS. THE GIRL FROM NOWHERE. JAZZ HEAVEN. GATEWAY TO THE MOON. You are a creature for whose use roadways and vehicles have been designed. Radio talks to you and plays music for you—song hits with titles incorporating the new slang—*Diga Diga Doo Diga Doo*—coming to you live from the famous Alpine Terrace. You move under the shadow of the newly completed skyscraper which is the temple of dawn. The city is shaped like your body. It has plazas and pools and moves to what has become your rhythm. Speeding until the lights are a gleaming blur. Swooping under bridges and out into the zone of foxtrot contests and dim-lit waterfront fish joints. Gun the motor until you reach the domain where astonishment is at the door. The territory of dangerous fun. Enter the darkness and it becomes bright. Light streams down in a neon waterfall. The time of the all-night saxophones has come. Dance bands jam at full throttle until your ears hurt. Showgirls step out of their robes at the Midnight Frolic. A theater critic becomes wittier the more martinis he drinks. All of them whipping themselves into a fever.

cornet solo in smoke

Where lights go dim the talk liquefies into moans and giggles. In nightclubs with secret passwords gangsters hobnob with socialites. Slumming parties. You have to watch your step in joints like that. Don't give your right name if there's a raid. Banjo player with fixed smile and neatly plastered-down thinning hair. Pinpoint eyes the sign of a hophead. A bald-headed businessman, his head fallen forward on a table. Fashionable ladies shrieking and cursing. Streams of confetti. Chorus line in grass skirts. Muted cornet solo in smoke. *It's only a shanty in old shanty town.* The fun they crank out is the latest thing since sliced bread. Plenty hot stuff. As if it was just a few minutes ago everybody managed to break loose from the Victorian Age. *Those days when they used to keep tabs on what everybody was getting up to.* A drunk college kid sounds off to his pals. *That's a lot of Puritanism! I've got my own life to live and I'm gonna live it my own way!* So what if the kid wants to go to Paris and live with an artist's model. It is the modern era and the young people need to be free. Hoodlums in the shadows case them as prospects for recruitment or blackmail or maybe a plain old stick-up. When the kid asks what happened to the girl he was buying drinks for he'll get the answer all right, from the guy with the face like a brick wall. *She took a run-out powder.*

emergency ward

The three nurses working the night shift in the emergency ward get to see the flip side of the currency. Some thrill. It falls apart along the seams after dark. People get out of line. Barely time to smoke a cigarette leaning against the wall under the No Smoking sign before the cases start rolling in. Maybe a bunch of sailors brawling over by the gas-house district. A drunk knocked down by a delivery truck and still yakking on the stretcher like nothing happened even though his leg is smashed all to hell. A homeless mother giving birth in an ambulance. A baby dead from inherited syphilis. A dapper young bootlegger with a bullet through his vest and still managing to flirt with the nurse before he blacks out. A pair of young doctors who sneak whiskey into the ward and make jokes about the fine figure on the girl that died half an hour ago on the third floor. The world-weary surgeon who finds it hard even to think about love anymore: a professional hazard. *I've taken them apart and put them together so many times that I don't suppose I have many illusions left.* They still talk about the specialist who ended up doing the procedure on his own father's brain tumor and couldn't save him. The intern who got in debt to gamblers and was nabbed for selling serum on the black market. And then there was the young doctor who only found out in the operating room that the girl hemorrhaging after a botched abortion was the nurse he got in trouble, that night—their only night—when they were both weak from seeing too much suffering in forty hours without sleep. *Tired of work and sweat and blood and pain.* Nurses understand more than they could ever tell. *The successful nurse is the one who keeps her mouth shut.*

a grid of dread

Reporters prop up the bar talking about tong wars in Chinatown, city councilmen on the take, wholesalers selling tainted milk and passing along the proceeds to the mayor's cronies. Gambling ships outside the two-mile limit where a troublesome customer might drop over the rail and never be heard from, and where underage girls find themselves locked in the staterooms of high rollers from out of state. Celebrated stage actresses caught in tête-à-têtes with Iberian gigolos. Shipments of dope picked up by sea plane two hundred miles off Montauk and distributed to mansions along the Sound. There is no end to the rackets—phony claims to unclaimed legacies, hoodlums muscling in on neighborhood tailor shops, fortune tellers setting their sights on susceptible widows, tabloid reporters passing as ministers or claims adjustors to purloin heartbreakingly private information and smear it across the front page—every substratum of chicanery from sideshow spielers and door-to-door bait-and-switch artists all the way up to the big-time connivers, the ones who prefer to be described as civic benefactors while they build concert halls and corner shares on the stock market and instigate foreign wars. People will put up with almost anything. It's cheap entertainment. *The public is like a cow, bellowing to be milked.* You can read about it tomorrow morning. On the street of a thousand alleys, storefronts masquerade as employment offices. The back room is a vice den. The city is a grid of dread. Awash in crimes for which there is no name and diseases for which there is no cure. *There's guys in this burg that could get you croaked for a dime, and for another dime prove you committed suicide.* They are in the shadows with their peepers trained on you, waiting to pounce at the first wrong step. You are heading for trouble the minute you step outside. Even what looks like a lucky break can go sour in a hurry. Keep walking past that swinging door. Don't let the character in the white suit buy you a drink. Everything happens before you have time to know it.

peculiar hobbies

In some precincts the pleasures are finer and more specialized, tailored for the people who know about foreign languages and paintings that look like nothing on earth. With the right sales pitch even a guy from the rackets might start investing in art. – *You ever see anything like that before? – Not since I been off cocaine.* A diva sings Wagner in the living room of a boiler manufacturer while the other guests doze or snuggle up to somebody else's spouse. Connoisseurs keep immeasurably precious porcelain behind glass. After hours you may find them at a dive in Greenwich Village where two boys dressed as girls sing a song about sailors. The swells come down in a taxi to have a look at the bohemian side of life. On another night you may find them in private mind-travel sessions with a swami who is now the toast of the sophisticated world. A cool customer who doesn't mind sampling the charms of the manufacturers' wives in between séances. They don't have to know that the closest he ever got to Tibet was Akron. The rubber capital of America seemed like a good locale for his rubber-check scam, until a carny mentalist clued him in that there were better ways to make a dishonest buck. The rich have their peculiar hobbies. Every now and again one of these birds is found murdered in his locked bedroom—shot through the temple while examining a rare edition of Baudelaire, in silk pajamas no less—and the cops have to make way for a cultivated detective who can tease out clues beyond the ken of any ordinary flatfoot. The guy can sight-read the inscriptions on Egyptian tombs. He can tell at a glance that the cipher on the swami's ring is a coded message of death. The solution to the code turns out to be right in the phone book, under L for Luxor.

Loose Ankles

the keyhole brigade

The latest from the keyhole brigade is all over the morning papers. The hints will get even spicier when evening shadows fall and America's savviest columnist pitches into his broadcast. The echo from a choo-choo train of chatter ripples through parlors and boudoirs. In front of a thousand mirrors the women apply the finishing touches to their makeup. They are on their way to an opening, or to a cocktail party, or to the cocktail party after the opening. Once they get there they will compare notes on their latest trips to Nice or Havana. There is bound to be frank discussion about marital secrets, roving eyes, afternoon trysts. They know it's a den of vipers but they're having too much fun to stop. That's what they tell themselves between the barbed comments about what other women are sporting and who other men are stepping out with and which one is going to end up with the beach property in Newport. *I've heard of platonic love but I didn't know there was such a thing as platonic jewelry.* From room to room drift fragments of talk about Hatha Yoga and the teachings of the Ascended Masters, vegetarianism, face lifts, the canals of Mars, Ming vases, contract bridge, depth psychology, health spas, pedigreed dogs, Elinor Glyn and Peggy Joyce, eugenics and monkey glands. *There's that quite good-looking young playwright, you know, the one from the South that writes so indecently!* Art connoisseurs who know everyone's secrets trade tips on the latest neo-mannerist masterpiece to come out of France. *That heavenly blue against that mauve curtain, doesn't that excite you?* The world's most renowned bridge expert, immersed in a game on the far side of the room, is not in the mood to mix in society. *I hate people who breathe on me, it spoils my concentration.*

problems of modern marriage

Those stuffed shirts with their stock market updates and their palaver about college football might be surprised to learn what their wives are up to with tango instructors while they're on Wall Street getting ulcers. Miniature golf may not be enough to soothe the problems of modern marriage. The husband neglects the wife for the secretary. The secretary is stepping out on the side with a bootlegger. The wife doesn't appreciate the husband because she has her mind fixed on money and status. Or else all she cares about are afternoon cocktail sessions and the Romeo waiting for her in a rented room while she finds an excuse to leave the apartment. *I can't endure being bored... I'm not bored with New York. I'm bored with life. To me, life is just an ashtray full of cigarette butts.* After the last guest leaves they can't avoid each other anymore and she lets him have it with an air of contemptuous sophistication. *Don't be so serious, Tony. What's a little divorce?* She takes off her earrings while he stares grimly at the carpet. His voice when he finally speaks is heavy, the wind's knocked out of him. *Think of all we've been to each other. I always thought you were happy.* Soon she will be cadging drinks in Bermuda off an Australian rancher who does not even realize she's a married woman. What does it amount to at the end, the husband will tell himself when he's standing alone in the empty living room. Everything was about business with him until things started to slip. The day he learns about his son getting an underage waitress in trouble will be one day too late.

He doesn't know yet that his daughter has just been given a jumbo-sized bracelet by the gambler who popped in supposedly by chance while she was modeling lingerie for an exclusive couturier. Slipped it on her finger before she could object, if she even felt so much like objecting. Even a good girl can end up at a road house while a gent with sharp clothes, a dapper pencil moustache, and slicked-back hair pours her a drink from a steel flask, murmuring as if to himself: *I like my olives green.*

the woman who considered herself cosmopolitan

There are forces at war inside modern women. Magazines publish cover stories about it. *Aren't women entitled to a thrill?* The woman who must decide between wanting children and having a career. The woman torn between honoring the bonds of marriage and being a liberated individual with needs of her own. *We've kicked the bottom out of that bucket known as the double standard.* Can she allow herself the freedom to love even if it shocks her best friend from boarding school? *It's disastrous to love. The awful possession that people exert over each other. Nobody has any rights about me except me.* There was always that difference between them even back in school. *Do you remember you were always afraid the boys would go too far, and I was afraid they wouldn't?* Young people don't know what they are getting into when they get married. They are bursting with novel notions. *No slaves to marriage around here!* Nobody can tell them a thing. They are crazy about each other and it is perfectly okay for a wife to work as well as her husband. *I'm a reader in a swell elegant publishing house. I start Monday. Isn't it great?* Nothing is more fun than mixing cocktails after they each come home from a day at the office. Only it never lasts. Once the unbridled masquerade parties and sodden games of cribbage start to lose their charm he will be groping her best friend in a taxi while she heads off on the night boat to Albany with her boss on an overnight "business" trip. This is the woman who considered herself cosmopolitan until she made the mistake of taking her partner at his word. All that talk about jealousy being outmoded in the modern world. *Marriage is so middle class.* He had been hard to resist. *I'd like to make love to you till you scream for help.* She ventured to use the word "promiscuous" as if it were an amusing novelty, not foreseeing the day when he would throw it in her face. *You told me you didn't believe in the old conventional morals.* It is always the woman who pays.

homebodies without a home

There is another couple, no longer young, a soft-spoken architect with thinning hair, a matron who long ago lost her taste for cocktail bashes. They love each other in secret and rendezvous in a faintly illuminated Chinese restaurant that none of their fashionable friends would ever poke their heads into. *We can't go on meeting in these terrible holes in the wall! Oh Babs dear, there must be some way out.* They can't marry because neither of their spouses will ever give them a divorce. It could have happened to anyone. A couple of homebodies without a home to share. Instead they have maintained their discreet twenty-year relationship—small exquisite pleasures and long glum regret for what might have been—memories of a few scattered weekends when they experienced what it might be like to be free. In the end, when it all comes out, their own children reject them. – *We're not ashamed. Our love is beautiful and we're proud of it.* – *Then why did you keep it a secret?* They must choose and the choice is self-evident. The customers around them joke and clink glasses while they look in each other's eyes for the last time. *We've had our happiness and now we have to pay for it.*

up against head winds

If I were free. He can't marry her. Or perhaps doesn't want to. No matter what he told her. *You mustn't take things a man says when he's tight too literally.* Even if she was the one who gave him the idea for the marketing concept that made him famous. His back-street woman who taught him all he knew about public relations. Estranged from her family by the threat of scandal and living now in another city, under another name. People make promises but the story changes when they find themselves up against head winds. She created her own design business but spends her nights alone. Happy to see his name in the newspaper. In the middle of a long empty evening the suitor she rejected shows up, the cultivated older man who admired her ideas from the beginning. He still has the letter that came back with no forwarding address. Barely legible from being carried around in his pocket for years. *I go from place to place and do the same thing—nothing. I've missed you more than I thought it was possible for one human being to miss another.* After she tells him how it is with her, he goes back to his hotel and blows his brains out. She'll be accused of murdering him, and the orphaned nephew she had looked after like a son when he was a baby—now a rising young prosecutor of stern humorless integrity—will all too effectively call down judgment on her. He grew up apart from her and can have no idea who she is. She would die before telling him. In fact, as it turns out, she does.

world without rules

There are fatal steps like kissing a married doctor. You enter a private world without rules. *Let's leave it at this. I'm afraid we've started something we can't finish.* If the blinds are up the coast is clear. The key is under the mat. *I'm probably wrecking my whole life and I can't help it. I don't want to help it.* They know it can't last forever and they don't care. The past always comes back anyway in the form of a boyfriend just out of the pen or back from the war. She never told anyone she had a husband in an institution. Never could have foreseen they would let him out. The psychologist who signed the release form was just going through the motions—he had problems of his own—didn't register the hollowness of the patient's laugh or the peculiar gleam persisting in the eyes even after years of treatment. The newspapers had said he died in the fire. There is no island on earth so remote that an unwanted lover can't find his way to it and grin as he hits on a terrific opportunity for blackmail. He never calls it that. *It's such an ugly word, baby.* She tries to imagine how life might have turned out if she hadn't given in that day. If she had waited the way you are supposed to. But it was already too late when she clutched his sleeve outside the boarding house and said *I've never done this kind of thing before.*

a certain amount of shattered glass

There is no time to wait any more. *Let's take our happiness now. None of us know what's going to happen next. Life's so short, so uncertain.* Nobody believes in the old barriers. Not in the cities they don't. Permission has been granted to do anything. *I want to be gay and have fun! I want to live while I'm alive!* No time to get stuffy about being engaged to someone else or not having your father's blessing. *Is that a way to welcome an old friend? Come over to my place, we'll have a couple of drinks and kick the gong around some more.* In a penthouse a man in a smoking jacket smiles knowingly and caresses a fur boa, sighing with pleasure at the resilient softness as he anticipates what is to follow. Partygoers sloshed on Veuve Clicquot—the men in tuxes, the women in sheer silk gowns—dive into pools, one after another, like they are trying out for the Midnight Frolics. *I'm in an orgy, wallowing, and I love it!* On all-night ferry boats bands wail and beer overflows on the sawdust floor. A sailor grabs the nearest girl even if it is going to end in a fistfight when her straight-arrow boyfriend objects. The night wouldn't be complete without a certain amount of shattered glass. The hotel lobby is jammed with bald-headed insurance men on a junket, goggle-eyed at the lineup of platinum-haired gold diggers. Young folks get the message and start sneaking smokes, stealing cars, breaking into locked liquor cabinets. *I may be able to scare up some liquid excitement.* They don't need more than a beat-up couch with broken springs, as long as they clear out before the old man gets back from the late shift. Take it where you can find it.

Fast Life

weird wrong turns

In one night in one nightclub twelve different life dramas play out. Step back and it looks like a network of interlocking cylinders. Or the kaleidoscope pattern that the girls in the floor show make in their finale, when they cluster together and blossom like flowers. No telling what is going to get handed out to who. One dies and another gets married. One ends up in a townhouse on Park and the other in a rickety tropical hotel where the rain never quits, downriver from where they load the manganese ore on barges. An overambitious piker gets cut down by the ricochets of the ambush he set up for someone else. The smartest operator in town falls backwards one afternoon into a vat of acid and not a soul will ever know where he disappeared to. *Nick took a powder I guess.* If a kid tags along to the party with the rest of the gang—looking to have some regular fun—somebody is sure to get arrested or run over before the night is done. *Stealing a couple of tires from a gas station didn't seem like that big of a thing. How was anybody supposed to know the night watchman had a gun.* No end to the weird wrong turns. Decent men with families to support get caught in a bind with no way out but to steal and cheat. Knowingly signing their names to doctored invoices. The nicest guy anybody ever met, just getting set up in life and his wife expecting, finds out he's been roped to be the cat's paw of mobsters peddling counterfeit pharmaceuticals. A well-fed little boy unwraps his birthday presents, ripping away the glittery ribbons with childish impatience, while kidnappers peer through the half-open window. Later that day they track him to the park where he sails his toy boat in happy obliviousness. The babysitter is in on it. It's not her fault if she loves a heartless guy.

it takes longer to tell than to happen

Anyway it is only a story. Told so fast that by the time you remember all the details it takes longer to tell than to happen. Forgot to mention about the babies switched because of the mistake with the tags at the clinic—and the planted evidence—the orderly conked on the head so a stool pigeon could take his place—the brother who came back unannounced from a South American rubber plantation right in time to be mistaken for his twin— and get plugged by a jealous girlfriend who was tired of being given the air—while the getaway van faked up as a furniture truck sat parked in front of the tenement at the exact moment that made it look like somebody ratted out a pal when really he didn't—and that the boss's cutie to make things even stickier had an afternoon rendezvous when she was supposed to be having tea with an old school chum who inconveniently for her alibi had been spotted leaving town on the daybreak express. Tried to tell him it didn't really happen the way it ended up looking— somebody must have pulled a fast one with the steamer trunks so that the one the cops jimmied open would turn out to have a day-old stiff in it—but some things you can't talk your way out of. That is always the way of it. Nothing but bad breaks all down the line. Get away with one thing and then they give it to you in the neck for the job somebody else pulled. A spin of the wheel. A pawn ticket slipped in the wrong pocket. Boys turn into killers. Girls turn into whores. Father loses his memory after a bad fall in the mining camp and never makes it home.

Mother waves goodbye. Cut to tombstone. Children on monkey bars in a playground. Cut to lineup of convicts in a prison yard. *Listen, kid. We're in a fast game. It doesn't last long. Why can't we have a little fun before it's over?*

box factory

In the shanties near the box factory is a place of mud and overalls and decrepit delivery wagons. Now and again someone works up the nerve to escape. She is tired of cringing from their clumsy paws. It is even worse when they crack their idea of a joke. Her life has been a vision of smokestacks. *Day after day, night after night, covering everything with the same soot, the same filth.* You can't even keep curtains clean. Things would have to be better where it doesn't smell of muck and turpentine. *I don't want love on the installment plan. A man and a woman want to get married here, what do they do? They go to the company for a house, they can't pick one that's nicer than the others because they're all the same. So they take Number 26—Number 26 to live in, to have their kids in, to die in.* Through the windows of a Pullman car she sees a snazzy couple waited on by servants in a private compartment. Once they're alone they uncork a champagne bottle, dance slow together, fall into an embrace while managing discreetly to close the blinds. *Looking in? Wrong way. Get in and look out!* Everything desirable has always just left town, the carnival that pulled out during the night before the sheriff had a chance to shut it down, the sales rep who knew he could find her a job (*you'd be a cinch*), the theatrical company headed for an opening in a ritzier locale. She's been chasing reflections of reflections. Now she's off to the place where the lights originate, the birthplace of excitement. It takes spunk but two years later she is a star on the White Way. She sings a French song to entertain the guests at her own dinner party. Those lessons paid off. It was worth it all to hear a diplomat compliment her on her perfect accent.

he never even found out

Everybody doesn't have such luck. A small-town girl, a little too desperate or a little too green, lets herself fall for a college boy. A swell young guy who knows all about tennis and the theory of heredity. He swears he's never met anyone like her before. When they walk along the riverbank, down among the willows, she points out the hiding places of her childhood that she never showed anyone. He tells her she was meant for something better than a dead-end burg. She believes everything he tells her. He probably believes it himself. It is his first time too. A polite kid the waitresses razz for the way he blushes when the talk gets salty. But he's learning fast. *You want to experience all of life, don't you?* That was the summer that seemed to go on forever. *Lock the door. I'm afraid someone might come in and take you away from me.* Next thing she knows his mother has talked him into a six-month tour of Europe. No forwarding address. So he never even found out about the baby she gave up for adoption to the nuns who shamed her with their unyielding eyes. She told them the father was dead. By then she is sharing a cold-water walk-up in the city with a hollow-eyed widow who does piecework on the kitchen table and coughs all the time while sewing buttons on dresses the girl could never afford to wear. Nobody to wear them for either. Her own folks won't talk to her anymore. When after months she musters the courage to look up the boyfriend's parents— barges past the officious butler when he informs her that no one is presently at home—they stall for time. The scheme is to arrange for a judge, who just happens to be a long-time business associate of the family, to have her railroaded on a trumped-up extortion charge. The guards straighten her out quick enough in the first roll call: *C'mon, c'mon, this ain't no beauty contest!* Badgered by rough matrons, she loses track of what's going on outside the walls, big city stranglings and corruption scandals, floods in Ohio and earthquakes in Nicaragua, the German war debt. But her wisecracking buddy on the outside isn't any wiser, to hear him tell it, after they finally release her into an unrecognizable world. *Me, I only read the sports and the funny pages.* You find the most decent people on the wrong side of the law. By the time she gets out there is no going back to the straight life.

a lot of slick talk

It's tough on either side of the line. Not many you can turn to for help. Men least of all. There isn't anything so low a man won't do it. *He's got ideas like all the rest of 'em.* The guy in the tailored white suit has a lot of slick talk backed up by exactly nothing. He can't handle it when his game goes sour on him. *You've got to believe me, baby. They took my yacht away and everything went to pieces.* That is when he will try any trick—fake his own suicide—tear up her return ticket—slip away from her after cutting a deal with a white slave trafficker from the outer peninsula. No matter how many times the truth comes out nothing will deter him from coming back and starting the routine all over again. His heartfelt pleading act is something to see. A lawyer once taught him the word "contrition" and tried to explain how to put it over in a courtroom. Not that he needed much explaining in that department. This is surely some craven and shameless character, a twisty-eyed weasel who laughs at any doctor or do-gooder getting in the way of his hustle. *Can that stuff, she's fed up with that line of hokum you preach.* By the time a girl gets wise to him it is always too late. The moment she breaks down, all the sympathy drains out of his eyes. *What's the idea of pulling this sob stuff. Have your hysterics and get it over with.*

the only thing that matters

One day she manages to catch sight of her baby in another woman's arms, on the lawn of a big suburban home in Connecticut. So desperate she'll sneak inside by pretending to be the housekeeper the agency sent over. Or start a career as the most popular female announcer on the radio just so she can broadcast messages to her lost child. If gangsters kidnap the kid she will jump out a window to foil them. She lives her life on the other side of a divide. Not much difference between rags and furs. In exile from the only thing that matters. *What chance has a woman got?* She will do anything to go back across the line—confess to a murder, commit one even—if for a single moment she can be reunited with her baby. No human law means anything anymore. A single strand of love connects her to the world. The rest is a stone desert. Hypocrites have been passing judgment on her since she started out. When the world finally looks in her direction—on a whim, on a cheap bet, because it makes a good story for the slimy characters that call themselves journalists—it is only to stage a spectacle of unbearable humiliation. *I think you can always get people interested in the crucifixion of a woman.*

too slow on the uptake

It is hard for her, being new in town and not having any friends. Her sacrifice is silent and never to be acknowledged. It might not have come to this if she'd been a little tougher at the start. Nowadays, with a different name, in dressing rooms and at private parties in hotel suites, she finds herself with women who know enough not to get hurt more than they already were. *All the gentleness and kindness in me have been killed. I found out that the only thing worthwhile is dough. And I'm gonna get it, see?* They feel for her even while they rib her. See to it that nobody leans on her too hard, and warn her who to stay away from. *The older ones are safer, if you know what I mean.* The girls might talk rough but they stick together when the pressure comes down. *When I was seventeen I found out there wasn't any Santy Claus. Don't ever let any man make a sucker out of you.* They have their tiffs, their territorial confrontations. *One more look at him with those bedroom eyes and I'll break your legs.* It happens all the time. Like when a kid from out of town auditions for the chorus line. *Looks like some carnival lost a good act.* They save the best lines for themselves. Why waste them on the men, since the lugs are mostly too slow on the uptake even to know when they are being razzed. *You're no crossword puzzle. You ain't got the brains you was born with.* Thickheaded galoots barrel through the world in their heavy bodies knocking obstacles out of their pathway until some thicker force comes along and knocks them down. The women have a good laugh about it in the wings and count their lucky stars that they aren't sleeping drunk under a bridge or holed up in a single room in a boarding house repeating the stories of old stage triumphs that nobody ever wanted to hear about in the first place: *I think that must have been the night Lincoln was shot.*

everybody knows everybody

Back in the old neighborhood there are couples who can't marry. On account of having no money. *Gee, Ma, I wish there was something else I could do besides jerk sodas for a living.* Young people watch their lives waste away while they look after their aging parents. One mother is like a saint, she wants to die so she won't be a burden on them. Another one—living next door for ten years and hasn't spoken a neighborly word all that time—clings to her son and accuses him of abandoning her only because he wants to walk his girlfriend home and linger on the stoop for a few precious minutes. *I've got a right to have some fun while I'm young.* Like stepping out to dance contests or sitting on a bench in the park. They ride the ferry back and forth. Share cigarettes to save money, look at the stars, dream big about decent jobs and sharp clothes and a washing machine. Have a good laugh about the old folks yelling from one side of the street to the other. Everybody knows everybody from the time they're born. Sometimes you can hear music at the bandstand after dark. *Gee, I'm stuck on that tune they're playin'.* One day they decide to take the plunge. Barely enough to scrape by. Washing and drying the dishes together in a fifth-floor walk-up. They can hardly carry on a conversation because of the couple yelling at each other in the next apartment or at the kids screaming in the alley. Maybe it would have been better to wait. *There's a lot of fun in love without having babies.*

no money in the jungle

Saturday night at the Orpheum they get a kick out of sitting up in the balcony and getting stuck into jungle pictures. The sound of those drums and birdcalls can set off a thrill. Not hard to imagine climbing into a tree house on a ladder made from vines. Living without clothes or even words. There is no money in the jungle. They don't smoke cigarettes there or take out the trash. A mischievous chimp swings from branch to branch. The clearing is some kind of paradise. Fruit off the trees and not a subway in sight. No need to get too worried about the witch doctors with faces painted like skulls or the ivory poachers leading captive natives on a forced march along a narrow ledge into the forbidden territory. All Tarzan has to do is give a yell and the elephants will come barreling through the trees to the rescue. Meanwhile as long as Tarzan and Jane have each other and their jungle hideaway everything is going to turn out hunky dory. They dive in the water from the tree house, splashing around naked, laughing like a couple of kids. The whole movie screen is a pool of water. You can almost feel it against your skin. Wet gleaming lily pads floating serenely and then a quick flash of a bare bottom. That would beat a tarpaper rooftop in August. *It could give a guy ideas.*

Blood Money

stake out an empty lot

The organ grinder's music gives them a sentimental glow. Until after a while it gets on their nerves. Or on his nerves to be exact. It's been like that since he lost the job in the packing department. Only because some gloomy Gus with an accent so thick you couldn't comprehend him half the time decided to make a speech about the workers being exploited. *Do you believe that slop they dish out to the masses? A load of bushwa.* Cranky as anything but you had to like his nerve. When some gorillas roughed up the poor sap, the boy stepped in and took a crack at one of them. Got bounced the same day. *A guy can't get a break anyway.* What do you expect in a neighborhood where children play craps and old women die without adequate medical care. *They had no business to put her out on the street when it was cold and wet.* His little brother is in a TB ward. Remember the young doctor with big ideals who used to work at the clinic? He got wise and moved uptown to Park Avenue. The kids on the playground plan their wars like little field marshals. Kids? Everybody here was born old. If they don't waste away in the back rooms of unheated tenements they grow up to be priests or racketeers. Here they don't play with toy blocks, they play with city blocks. Stake out an empty lot as command center, a warehouse basement as munitions dump. Post lookouts along a network of broken windows. They throw stones at interlopers, snatch coal from trolley cars to bring home to the mother who can no longer handle the stairs. She doesn't really want to know where they've been.

not a trace of you lingers

Mister Benedek who runs the cigar store reads books behind the counter. *The Outline of History. The Origin of the Family* by Engels. A gruff guy but when no one is looking he'll give a toy to a sick child. A cheap enough trinket, the one he'd seen her looking at day after day through the window. He tells the little ones what Cossacks were. But the kid he remembers best, the one who showed signs of interest—*a boy with sense, not like the rest of those hooligans*—stopped showing up. He is making a name for himself in the rackets. The city doesn't remember anybody's childhood for long. You get so lost not a trace of you lingers, even on streets where you grew up. Except for that one girl who never got married and never forgot. Worn out now, carrying heavy buckets up three flights of stairs, alone now, still living in the apartment down the hall. – *Nothing changed, Johnny, I just got older.* – *The whole world got older.* They find the spot where they scratched their names in the thick lead paint of the basement wall. Their secret meeting place. She shows him the pearl button he gave her at recess in fifth grade. Her hands were more delicate than he can bear to remember, before she went to work in the button factory. They still are, he tells her. They both know it's a lie. She will never call the police no matter what.

silent glares

Toward closing time when the cold wind sweeps through the alley the dried-up geezers crowd around the radiator in the back room. One old guy, half-pickled, paints a word picture of the old country of palm courts and gypsy violins. Where the barber and the baker traded neighborly greetings or extravagant good-natured insults, and the girls in bright scarves blushed at the gallantries of roguish students. An old woman wove quilt patterns while she hummed the traditional lullaby. And the noodles, nothing like them. But this was a lie, wasn't it? Half the time they were afraid of their shadows back there. Hussars with shiny buttons patrolled the square. The lamplight on the buttons looked like menacing flames. The men of the village could do nothing. It was left to the old women to condemn the tormentors with silent glares. The violinist couldn't even protect his fiancée from the degrading insults of those arrogant monsters with their epaulettes and hunting parties and all-night gambling sessions. The degenerated products of ancestral military hierarchies. Whipped at dawn if the jacket wasn't straight. Honest girls selling their bodies to get a ticket of safe conduct. Young men who protested sent off to slave labor and never seen again. Russia, Austria, Prussia, same difference. It had been going on like that for centuries. Brutes knocked over candlesticks on the banquet table as they egged each other on to more wildness. The mazurka music made them crazy. Drink made them cruel. Tailors were born to be oppressed. Only with the last gleam in his eye he still had the satisfaction of telling them their days were numbered.

it is always some gimmick

Then they arrive in the new land to find the brutes are the same as the ones they left behind. Everything is the same only with different tailoring. No gold buttons. Gold spittoons maybe. *America gonif!* Here they elect the thieves instead of having them fixed in place since the crowning of Charlemagne. The politicians snap their suspenders in public, stand on a platform under a banner keeping up a steady stream of twenty-dollar words while fireworks go off. Big men: the public never gets to see the moments when they sweat with fear in their clubhouses because they think for a minute they might lose their grip on whatever grift they're running, sold out by some other grifter. No guts when it comes to swallowing their own medicine. No matter who is in charge it is always some gimmick for taking coins out of the mouths of the poor. Everybody wants to be a big shot. *Real mahogany, carpets up to your ankles, dollar cigars. Special blend. I have them made for me in Havana.* Filing into the inner sanctum where they carve up the take. *You've got a chance to be a big noise around here.* Young recruits in snap-brim hats. Straight out of reform school. *Up on your feet, apes.* As long as they don't step out of line. *Any mug that don't think so will be treated to the swellest funeral that ever stopped traffic. Won't think it's so funny then.*

black cars tear zigzags

Taking over a town can go to your head if you let it. Especially when it turns out to be so easy. The chumps never saw it coming. *Do it first, do it yourself, and keep on doing it.* Go block by block and before you know it you have things under control. Run everything like a business. Funny how it feels like being kids again. Rolling trucks down highways, smashing them into each other, running ambushes from around the corner. Windows shatter in the crossfire. Black cars tear zigzags through the street. If a guy gets wise knock him dopy until he understands the message. A couple of hours in the back room does the trick. *You're soaking up plenty of grief, kid, why don't you give yourself a break?* Take aim at apartments from rooftops. When the light goes on they have a clear shot at the retired custodian in the armchair with his evening paper who is supposed to give the DA eyewitness testimony next day. Next on the roster is the front page reporter who forgot what side his bread is buttered on. Everything has been carved up on a map. Napoleon planned his campaigns exactly the same way. *Those guys were born to be drilled at one o'clock Tuesday and that's when they got it.*

the world is in your pocket

From the start they figured to set themselves up in nightclubs. Everything free because they own the joint. The jazz band keeps it pumping as long as they tell them to. The dancers are their personal harem. Give the mayor and the rest of the city hall mugs a ringside seat for the floor show and send them a bucket of champagne as a symptom of good will. Tell the stuffed shirts to stick around for the apache number and watch their eyes go bleary as they swill the liquor. Fresh off the boat and I'm the queen of Herzegovina. Those birds wouldn't know the difference if it was made in somebody's outhouse. *I never use the stuff, you know that. I have to know what's going on all the time.* The operation has to be run like a Ford plant, from the drop-off points along the river to the suburban warehouses. It is all based on timing. *You've got a sweet racket here, maybe I can teach you a few new wrinkles.* The city teaches you how to be sharp and finally you are sharper than the city. After that you don't have to take orders. The world is in your pocket, along with a private army in black fedoras. Those lugs move when you say move. *Just stay in circulation, and lay off that snow till this gets cold.* Not ever telling them more than they need to know. *I do other people's thinking for them and make them like it.* Aldermen take their hats off. The door to the private office has frosted glass like a bank.

it wasn't even his gun

The tough guy rolls downstairs after they plug him. Should have learned to keep his trap shut. He can't quite close his hand over whatever he was trying to grasp. *A handful of clouds. I mean the kind that comes out of a .38 automatic.* The fall guy who didn't actually pull the trigger finds himself up against a stretch in Leavenworth. Time off for good behavior until he gets blamed for another con's escape attempt. The weak ones go to pieces. A greenhorn who wasn't cut out for the hard life gets locked up on account of losing his nerve in a hold-up. He let the gun go off when he shouldn't have and a bank guard happened to get in the way. He was only a lookout. It wasn't even his gun. He was holding it for the pal who happened to go missing with the loot just when the coppers were closing in. Another one of these amateurs, a clean-cut youth doing five for embezzlement, goes frantic after a couple of months. *You don't know what it's like in here. Every hour, every minute is torture. I'll go crazy.* Shouldn't have let himself get caught with his hand in the till, all so he could pay for his wife's frocks. *When a dress costs over a hundred bucks it's a frock.* It drives him nuts to see her on the other side of the wire screen. *If only I could kiss you.* One Thursday she doesn't show up. Working overtime at the secretarial job she manages to hold down even though she's never typed a letter in her life. *She doesn't know whether a typewriter is animal or vegetable.* He stares at her photo until his cellmate starts riding him. *Think she'll be waitin' around for you at the end of four years? Say, lay off the pipe.* Next morning they find him hanging from the bars.

those last two seconds

The big door slams. He has entered another country and he can taste the difference right away. Other rules here. Maybe no rules. In the country of lost men the guards are lost too. Even the warden can't call the shots, once the governor and his cronies stick their noses in it. *They all want to throw people into prison, but they don't want to provide for them once they are in.* Johnny is the toughest guy on the yard but he has to admit it: *The warden's not such a bad egg.* Johnny watched him stride into the yard where the men were lined up—his first day on the job, he needed to make an impression—and move down the rows looking each of those mugs straight in the eye. Men who have their code of conduct laid down thick like the shadows of iron bars. They assess their own penalties and administer their own punishments. Can be shoved but not owned. Would rather die than eat dirt. Judges and politicians know nothing about these things. Life gets measured by a different yardstick inside. It gets so real that the memory of the other side of the walls seems hollow and washed out. A cheap whiskey dream. Johnny is an ace, a right guy to the end. Walks the last mile because he wouldn't rat out his worst enemy. *You can't squeal in stir.* Now the time for remembering is all used up. While they strap him down he's thinking about the son he'll never see. The chaplain is laying on some last-minute spiritual counsel and Johnny can't be bothered to give him a comeback. *Too late for words, padre.* The warden looks sick inside as he tells the reporters: *This is simply an organized manifestation of the will of the taxpayers.* Reporters have front row seats. Some of them seem to think it's funny. *There ain't gonna be any legs in this show.* Now is when they pull the switch. Prison is where you learn what a man is supposed to be, but by the time you learn it you don't have even two extra seconds to spell it out. Nothing left but what is in the eyes before they go blank. Somebody said your whole life goes by in those last two seconds.

Doorway to Hell

into the back country

This is when he wishes he could be walking down that long lane into the back country. Back when he hardly knew there was such a thing as cities. Deep enough into it to see a plough horse against the horizon. Cabin smoke beyond the ridge. Just in time for supper at the homestead, Ma ladling out soup, Pa folding his hands to say grace. Will they recognize him. The scrawny gray dog surely will. Beautiful in that country until somebody misbehaves. The preacher never read the part about forgiveness in that book he likes to quote from. Gossip slips across backyard fences. It gets hard even to walk into a store to buy turnips, facing those judging faces at every step. Scout out crannies to get clear of them. A shack with cobwebbed windows where nobody goes. There are hard-luck foundlings back there. A child who ran wild in the settlements cast out for that Indian strain. She broke horses as if it came naturally. Distant harmonies from fields and cabins. Old rugged church in deep woods. A fog rising out of the valley. Blind man singing a hymn among the pines at night. So old he can remember what everybody else chose to forget, the cruelties never written down. For a while in the thick darkness he has the road to himself. Down to the crossroads marking the invisible barrier between settlements. Chain gang country. Vigilantes work part time as guards at the prison farm. Deliberately goad their prisoners to violence. Flames reflected on sweaty brows. Wavering silhouettes of shotguns against the wall. If the runaway makes it back to town where would he go.

Cornered in a barn or thrown in a jail to be burned. The storekeeper and the sheriff pass the moonshine back and forth across the scarred wooden table. Bent over in the convulsions of their laughter.

streets made of stares

The runaway heads further into swampland. The land gets more watery and then is delta. Warm sea stretches toward offshore havens. Islands of tropical torpor out past the fog. Bodies of land too small to figure on any chart, far removed from the regular shipping lanes. The coordinates deliberately miscopied in case anybody should get too curious. Shore lights rigged to lead astray. Islands run as private zoos stocked with hybrid vipers and fanged predators. Laboratories for the creation of new species. Exotic skin grafts. Trafficking in body parts ostensibly to formulate a new serum. Human blood to be mingled with other species. Prisoners bundled in crates like so many wild beasts. Whispers whistle through the cane brakes. The moon falls aslant on the deserted verandah. *Once a man gets this far from the mainland he is going to have the devil's own time getting back.* The years become a long rum-soaked barbecue. *There's some things you don't care to remember.* On the farther shore the cargo will be handed off to a degenerate shipping agent. A horse-drawn wagon moves slowly from the harbor, the mutilated face of its driver revealed for a second by a lamp in a window. He lurches forward guided by the glow. The woman is to be swept up as she returns to her dressing room, moments after her song ends. Silenced with a chloroform-soaked rag before she can tell what is happening. The signal had been a nod from the cloaked man in the side street whose hat brim masks his eyes. Along the seams of every city are these shadow zones: docks, manholes, catwalks, concealed delivery entrances, disused warehouses, dripping tunnels, basement-level rat-infested loading platforms. Everything finally ends up here. Peel away the bright images of a protected life—the bashful students out on their first date—the child's birthday feast—the world-famous biologist welcomed home by his family— and find these other pictures, discolored under layers of bandage. The heart of the town is encircled by streets made of stares. Close your own so as not to be seen. The innocent have nothing to be afraid of.

behind a wall of mountains

Lookout points dot the map. To cross unwittingly into restricted territory is to submit to surveillance by agents disguised as waiters or uniformed porters. At a remote location their master has a hole he stares through—a globe—a screen of flickering signals. Behind a wall of mountains breached by a pass known only to his initiates. Messages arrive from the tents of fortune tellers or makeshift waterfront taverns. A nod will do the trick, or a single phrase in a nearly extinct Central Asian dialect. Undetected he travels back and forth across the barrier. He attends embassy receptions and smiles with impeccable politeness at the white-haired gentleman whose nephew has vanished in Fez. He professes sympathy in tones that would deceive no alert observer, if only among these complacent functionaries there were one such. The covert maneuvers by which he directs coming events makes possible his much remarked ability to predict them. They should have taken him at his word. *I do not foresee the future, Sir Charles, I construct it.* From his fastness he has for years studied every weak point of the interlopers whose imperial bluster substitutes for anything like an ordering intelligence. They claim superiority to a people whose culture was ancient when England was home to rude painted brutes. He nourishes a contempt so exquisitely molded as to resemble a work of art. Life is for him a game to be played at the highest level of refinement and for the highest stakes. With a coldness those of the West can scarcely envision—a coldness not of indifference but of the most acute concentration—he considers in what sequence to stage the dismantling of their world.

a cherished poison

In beauty is the birth of cruelty: the beauty of certain masterpieces too perversely delicate to warrant anything but contemptuous dismissal from the herd of coarse-minded critics and unscrupulous art dealers. Oafs insensible to the needs of a genius pulled taut like the shrillest violin string. The merchants, the impresarios, the pilferers and gluttons have earned their reward. To some it has already been meted out, in secret. No one will know what was his sorrow at being forced to endure the banter of illiterate draymen. The strangler carries his grief inside like a cherished poison. He conceives of his hands as implements of artmaking. The world will come to accept the purity of his dream, a beauty forged through the most extreme sacrifice. *Wasn't it Nietzsche who said that unendurable pain merges into ecstasy?* His face is a waxy mask that hides what the fire did when a gallery owner burned his greatest creations for the insurance money. A tongueless hunchback—his only companion in this life— waits for him in the courtyard. In a basement hideout his mind has laid out a magnified model of itself by means of interconnected vats and viaducts reaching almost to the ceiling. The acid baths are preliminary passageways leading toward the dawn of *a new world such as you are scarcely fit to imagine.* The insensitive policemen force the lab door open as the half-nude body of the abducted singer is being lowered slowly into the nullifying liquid. He picked her out because she looked exactly like the woman whose portrait has been hanging all these years in a private shrine for his mournful incommunicable worship.

a mystery

Who sat for that portrait? That is a mystery that the chief of detectives would give half his retirement pay to solve. Could it have been her that a certain naive young man—naive enough to fancy himself a model of cosmopolitanism—had glimpsed so many years earlier, as if in another life, from his cheap balcony seat at the opera? Or was it another, whose bone structure resembled hers so precisely that she might well pretend to be her? A woman wearing artful imitations of her favorite jewels and affecting the hint of an accent not native to her? He was drawn at first by the glint of her silvery wrap. The strains of *Thaïs* faded into inaudibility as her glance—*like banked fires*—penetrated him across that gulf. The schoolboy he was then could not yet imagine the degree of suffering that brought her there, along an obscure path leading from the warehouses of Chicago to the houseboats of Mandalay. She was never to be made a pawn again. Never again to be the only woman in the hotel, holed up in her room for days subsisting on gin to the point of delirium, on the only island with no extradition treaty, her only company the long-term fugitives in residence spitting betel juice on the splintered floor and staring at her as she descended the staircase. *Nothing but men, dirty rotten men.* In a voyage that never ends she goes from nowhere to nowhere with an air of contemptuous finesse. *We call them suicide passengers.* The past is indecipherable. The future is a stretch of arid scrubland, or perhaps a malaria-ridden jungle to be re-entered like the convent where so many years ago she learned to trace the letters of a foreign alphabet. But not before she has exacted punishment on that declining generation of property holders, with their dinner parties where inadequate breeding is exposed to merciless ridicule, their dowagers capable of any moral crime to prevent their milksop sons from marrying beneath their imagined dignity. To those with no mercy no mercy will be shown. But not before she has had her fun. *Some might call it irregular or even immoral.* Under her tutelage fashion goes mad and anything anything becomes imaginable. Women in dresses resembling metallic sheathes—high society profligates bent on replicating the pagan shamelessness of fallen empires—mingle on the gleaming border of a haughty and lascivious utopia. Silver is fleshy here and flesh silvery. *No ideals, no illusions, only desires.* Her unwavering apartness shifts the gala off center by an intimacy she conjures but will never fulfill. She leads the captivated toward a sacrificial altar set off by rococo tiles and florid folds.

palm trees in shifting light

There was a time when she learned to speak flawless Bulgarian for clandestine communication with the wrong side of the frontier. She could already sing songs in French with a mix of teasing insouciance and icy indifference: *Lorsque tout est fini... Quand se meurt votre beau rêve...* She is French, in part. She is part everything, she liked to joke, until it stopped being a joke. She can make every man to whom she addresses a word feel abashed. Humiliated in fact, at the end if not the beginning. Even a diplomat as perfectly at ease in Tsarist court circles as in the bordellos of Smyrna (*not much difference, if the truth were told*) will finally stammer for words. Astounding him with her knowledge of what was contained in those classic leatherbound volumes he inherited but has scarcely read. The brutality of her early years unknown except to the man chiefly responsible for it, when she finally reveals her birth name to him as they prepare to consummate their private orgy. In the meantime, alone for a few minutes, she leans on the balcony railing and stares at the palm trees in shifting light. A firing squad is nothing, weighed in the balance against her joy as she stands with the doors flung wide to the breeze. She raises a champagne glass to the moon. The general's bedroom is dominated by murals of imperial Roman women with gigantic golden bracelets around their naked hips. They bathe in milk and afterwards are caressed by slave girls. Through the windows can be heard the tumult of approaching rioters. She has no difficulty pretending to be entertained right up to the last moment. After she has completed what she came to do—having allowed herself one silent moment to contemplate his body fallen back in the chair, his face made instantly grotesque by the action of the poison—she lets herself be taken prisoner without resistance. Disdains the chaplain's Bible reading. Himself half in love with her, pathetically pleased that she had seemed to flirt with him on her way to the courtyard. She will request a last cigarette—but here the account goes blank. No official record will remain of what unknown agency has left a side door open, and a moment's inattention to allow her to slip through it, whether out of pity or passionate attachment or a toss of the coin. Or is it merely a judgment deferred, as she sets off with perverse confidence into the contaminated jungle from which she can hardly hope to emerge. What has she ever known but this insistent forward stride, once through shifting backdrops of smoky dens and fetid alleys, navigating the thoroughfares where her path was crossed by swindlers and police spies, and now into the heart of what she must finally be engulfed by.

along the edges of the uncharted world

Few have ever made it through that wall of howls and hisses. Fever hangs from the branches. Beast eyes glow in shadows. Coiled forms slither. *They love, they hate, they kill.* Everything alive is in a fatal trap, bait for an unseen predator. At every turn the bewildered explorer seems to leave another part of himself behind, hoping some scarred and ragged remnant will be left if he ever reaches the next trading post. The post turns out to be a pile of ashes beyond which the vegetation thins out and disappears entirely. The desert purifies or annihilates. Or purifies and then annihilates. The surviving members of the mission no longer remember what the mission was. To make a map? To locate a rich vein of exploitable ore? To excavate the burial grounds of a vanished civilization? Every form of authority disintegrates under the blinding sun. Babbling cowards have already dropped to the sand. Once they lost their pith helmets their brains fried. Only those beyond hope—outcasts stained definitively by some early disgrace—can sustain a swagger in the face of extinction. They have come so far beyond the picnics and athletic contests of their youth, when everything seemed a glorious game. Unshaven and in rags they advance gaily into the howling wasteland. No longer caring whether they find their way out, they roar like feckless drunken cadets. The stragglers, or what is left of them, limp forward in trance. The sunburnt plain makes pictures of imaginary rivers. It would seem that nobody is going to save them. Yet all along the edges of the uncharted world, sea planes are circling, looking for a trace of the lost expedition.

Turn Back the Clock

an erratic crackling sound

Modern civilization is audible long before the city comes in sight above the water line. It starts as an erratic crackling sound breaking through in mid-ocean. Wireless messages on shipboard are already announcing a gala reception for the survivors of the lost expedition. Rows of telephone operators jam prongs into outlets as the scoop spreads from bureau to bureau. Reporters bark out ready-made front page copy to the city desk. Tabloids roll from the presses straight into news trucks. Announcers rattle off bulletins as quick as they come over the wire. Klaxons clear traffic for the mayor's convoy as it speeds toward the harbor. The survivors are transported uptown under cascades of ticker tape. It is the story of the century: Rescued Heroes Come Home. Tickets to the party are awarded as prizes in a radio quiz game. (*The explorers lost their way in the largest desert in the world. Can you name it?*) As the fete gets underway they are swamped by press agents and advertising reps. Bathed and barbered and decked out in identical white dinner jackets, they try not to flinch from the barrage of flashbulbs. A portly adman in a tux, fuddled with Manhattans, wants to name a brand of soap after them since they got away so clean. *I was going to write the great American novel and now I'm writing slogans to make morons like you buy things you don't want.* Chorus girls in grass skirts drape them with flowers while the ukulele ensemble breaks into swing rhythm.

Should you ever take a notion
That you want to cross the ocean
Just take a steamboat to Hawaii land

The girls couldn't be happier. They got the job only that morning. It is the first work they've had in a dog's age and they are ready to let it rip. *If I felt any better I'd be a national menace.*

calendar pages flipping

If the rescued commander of the expedition is no longer as haggard as when they hauled him on board, he still looks a little unsettled by his surroundings. He can hardly understand the lingo anymore. They were gone so long. The war had barely ended when they set out and now it seems it's barely remembered. The years went by like calendar pages flipping. A vision of numbers changing in a mad blur. He had a home country once, before he took up exploring, but it was never like this. In the place he started out from—a town you'll never find on a map— time was never much of a consideration. Back there it hardly seemed to budge. Now from the looks of it there is nothing but time. Enough to throw it around without a care for wasting it. So often in the wilderness he and his buddies wondered what it would be like to go home. Never thought they'd miss a place they were once pretty hot to get away from. But the country they grew up in must have dissolved while they were absent. How poky was it back there? So poky a person could stare out the fly-specked window of the bus depot and watch nothing happening for longer than it took to go halfway across a continent. News came from far off and the mildewed newspaper cuttings of memorable disasters and athletic feats were pasted to barn walls like relics. Busybodies clucked behind curtains about tiny infractions of the local dress code. Young men bragged about roadhouse exploits never to be written down, triumphs they would repeat endlessly in their cups to their dying day. The local dignitaries held an inaugural ceremony for the town's first parking meter and the *Gazette*'s photograph of the historic occasion was later tacked to the post office bulletin board. It didn't amount to much—maybe that was why he was so quick to sign up on the first ship sailing for parts unknown—but it was really all the commander can call to mind about the native land he still gets misty-eyed about, even if it has been years since he set foot on its shores. In his bones he can still feel the hangover from a thousand and one nights of simmering itchiness, summer heat waves that lasted forever. He remembers rained-out afternoons when people were too tired to get up off the sofa. That was when the conversations of the old folks trailed off into hums and sighs and then stopped dead, almost with relief, when they couldn't think of a thing to add. Wish it would warm up a little. I saw your friend Willis the other day downtown looking all spruced up. What time did you say it was? Seems like everything gets more... I don't know what. It settled down into a silence like an unfurnished room in a boarding house, or a drifter staring down an empty road, or downtown Sunday night with all the shops closed, or the field in dead of winter back behind the line of shacks.

guilty curiosity

There was even, not long ago, a time before automobiles. Odd to think of it. Before telephones even. Almost beyond remembering, how those stiff collars and dark scratchy fabrics felt to a child's hand rummaging through closets and drawers. Elderly men with prim cadaverous faces and grandmothers propped up with stays and laces murmured and curtsied in a waxworks world. The women did not paint their faces. Would not dream of such a thing. Suppose there are some still but not hereabouts. Sunday School teachers wrote maxims on chalkboards— *Folly loves the man who holds sanctity in contempt*—and condemned defiant sluggards to write them fifty times. How scared the children felt sometimes but never said it. They found secret amazement through *Little Journeys in Bible Land*, in a country of deserts and streams, goats and gullies, shepherd's crooks and woolen robes. The children lingered with guilty curiosity on the engraved image of flames bursting from the sky. God was punishing a city for its luxury and drunkenness as its terrified sinners, men and women in loose shimmering garments—some still clutching golden goblets—tried to outrun the lightning. Forbidden things were hidden in pictures. Otherwise their world was a round of chores. Every object was a reminder about somebody doing something, mops and brooms, chisels and shovels, schoolroom charts of the multiplication table, inkwells nested in desk tops, ledgers stacked behind grilled windows, fishing rods and hunting rifles, needles and tweezers and pincushions, small vials of liniment oil and witch hazel, rags and scrapers and hooks. Instruction and examination led to embarrassment and in the worst case punishment. In the intervals between you waited only for the anticipated moment, at dusk or in the night or at the earliest hour when the grass was still wet, to sneak an unscheduled truancy. Then came games and dares and shrieks. They ran around in the half-light and got their feet soaking wet. Not scared, just laughing out of control.

nothing but air and rock

Home was to be escaped from. Some stepped into dark theaters to watch pictures of horses riding across ridges. A lone figure on a mesa peered down across bare flatlands toward a distant blaze. He lassoed a crag and swung to the far side of the crevice. Cruel rustlers with scarves over their mouths tied people up and abandoned them in cabins. Storms knocked down trees as a lost homesteader tried to find his way out of the forest. A fragment gleamed in the creek where a grizzled miner was panning. Then came the disorderly hordes swaggering down the muddy street who in their drunkenness threw chairs through the windows of barber shops. A wheel came loose and a chuck wagon smashed against the edge of a canyon. A bandit in an immense sombrero cracked a whip. A girl in a gingham dress cowered against a wall. She had come from back east after her father sent word of his illness. And now everybody wanted to get their hands on the scrap of paper that showed where the mine entrance was. Gunshots from an unseen marksman brought down the marauders before they could have their way with her. It was a good thing she had a cowboy for a friend. Now that there was no longer anything to fear or conceal, the two of them rode away and kept on riding. Dust whirled across open spaces that went on forever. There was nothing but air and rock.

The Crash

something died inside

The boys no sooner got out of school than they had to go marching to Europe. *We were told we were fighting for our country. All that band-playing and flag-waving and general hysteria. Maybe we were kidded.* Nobody back home could picture what it was like. Flying a crate over enemy lines and catching flak. Burnt up in mid-air. Teenage boys blown apart in trenches as they were reading a letter from home or lighting a third cigarette on that same match that gave the Huns time to spot them. Driven mad by the waiting even before they went over the top into a wall of machine-gun fire. Never did figure out what they were doing there in the first place. *Somebody shot somebody so now we all got to go out and get shot.* Some lost their minds, some crashed their planes, some got hooked on the injections for the pain. A few developed a taste for the action. There was nothing quite like swooping down from the clouds to chalk up another kill. *The prettiest piece of stick-work you ever saw... Above 'em and below 'em and around 'em all at the same time.* After a while something died inside. Some never went home at all. They would see them in the small hours in Paris cafés, clowning around, smashing furniture, running outside to jump in the Seine—*making quite a spectacle of themselves*—laughing continuously because if they stopped they might never laugh again. And the rest? They came back to fast money and gyrating dancers and the crossfire of hijackers. *I went to France to make the world safe for democracy, and what did we do? We made the world safe for the advertising business and the bootleggers and the gangsters.* Came back as hopheads and head cases. Came back with short fuses and itchy trigger fingers. They taught him to kill and now they were going to kill him for doing more of the same. Came back as a cynical drunk telling the woman who loves him that he has no love to give. *It's always two o'clock in my life.*

like knocking back a stiff one

The big speed-up came. Must have been brewing while they were away. *Don't be surprised to find there's been some changes made.* The bandleader signals and the horns blast in fast unison, clarinets wailing on top, drums banging furiously. A couple of lovebirds on a spree scream as the roller coaster plunges toward the next curve. A roadster on a midnight joy ride purrs at top velocity down a country lane toward the twinkling lights of a lakefront casino. An alarm clock clangs and a slim blonde in silk lingerie pops out of bed. It won't take long for something to happen. It hits you with a wallop like knocking back a stiff one. A slap in the face. Or a kick in the pants if you need it. Some master of ceremonies is yelling through a megaphone. There isn't time anymore for anything to take time. *Ten minutes ahead is about as far as I ever look.* Ready to start on a dime. *Snap into it.* The money is moving too. The numbers spin in dizzying circles. Wheels on top of wheels, click upon click. Thin strips of paper stream without stopping. Hoarse voices bark stock orders. *In a market like this a second is a lifetime and a minute is eternity.* Clerks on their lunch break bet their week's salary on a hot lead. Soda jerks cluster around pay phones to catch stray tips they can buy into on margin. Men coach their wives to flirt with dinner guests to tease out investment secrets. *I solicit tips with my charm and you convert them to money. Sometimes I'm half sick with shame over the things I do.* At a fancy dinner party the hired help gather around the keyhole to catch what brokers say over cigars. *You remember that terrific killing in Cobra Copper.* They thought they died and went to heaven. *Spending dough like a sailor in a dream.* In their dreams. Anyway the dream won't last long. *Money's a little bit tight everywhere.* Maybe all the fun was a wild-eyed rumor. By the time the word spreads to the hinterlands the party is already over.

petal upon petal floated down

How long ago was that? Last month? A hundred years? They had walked into a darkened palace for a few hours. Luxurious like the depths of a mystic Egyptian tomb. When they emerged everything had changed. Maybe it was more than a few hours. They lost track of time in the endless organ drone. Lost track of themselves, which was the idea in the first place. One picture melted into the next. Petal upon petal floated down into the meandering stream. Chariots swept across wide empty plains. Messages were delivered on scrolls. *The crescent moon from out the Syrian hills has flung aloft its livid signal. The day of sacrifice has come.* Within the gates of pagan temples unclad maidens bowed down at the place of immolation. By firelight the glittering blades of bronze weaponry cast ominous shadows. Goat-footed idols stooped over the bound bodies of gauzy-robed beauties. It was an opium vision orchestrated by a bearded hypnotist within the stone tower to which he lured unsuspecting debutantes. As they went further into the dream the organ music grew somber. No words were needed for everything they imagined they caught sight of among the folds and flurries. Couples in flowery bowers could not resist each other. Blinking eyelashes beckoned into brocaded interiors. A kiss filled the whole screen. They were transfixed by images of eddying water swirling toward a dark abyss. They bathed in wordless splendors. They were shocked when the music stopped and even more shocked when they stepped outside.

the final cocktail frolic

On street corners scavengers are peddling the cast-off debris of a suddenly vanished world. *Things haven't been so lucky for me since they had to close the plant down.* Solid locations evaporate without warning while the phonograph continues to play the songs about cherries and bananas and blue skies and a four-leaf clover. *You can't get enough dough in your cash register to buy a kitten cream.* When the moving men start to roll the piano out of the parlor, she tries to block them even though she knows they have to eat too. *It's pretty tough to lose your job in times like these.* She wears out her heels on streets where no sign gives welcome. *NO JOBS TODAY. NO HELP WANTED.* She might end up hiding out in the department store after closing time, dodging the night watchman so she can sleep in the model home display. A banker goes down on his knees for the bailout that even his father-in-law refuses. *Assets? What assets? You haven't got any! You've been making loans on worthless collateral.* The final cocktail frolic breaks up in the shadow of a hard-luck investor taking a dive from a high window. Another blows his brains out in the men's room of a swanky hotel. Suicide can be a way of making it up to the people you let down. Clear the way for their happy ending. The beloved father who drank too much and made bad investments can solve everyone's problem by flying his private plane into a mountain.

the only man who could save everybody

Or else—when there are no board members left to bully into submission, no bankers left to blackmail into floating dubious loans, no competitors left to crush with brutally unfair tactics, no mid-level managers left to shame into jeopardizing their marriages by working overtime every night, no loyal assistants left to exploit sexually for years on end while still finding time to take advantage of an intern fresh out of high school, spiking her drink at a penthouse pool party if necessary—it is a way to take the only possible exit, from the top floor of the skyscraper that was his own creation, the embodiment of his obsession. Or was he pushed? Nothing short of murder, a resentment long repressed suddenly surging up, can have cut short the forward march of the irresistible Napoleon of retail. *There's no room for sympathy or softness. My code is smash or be smashed.* Seductive and cruel, the picture of hard-shelled arrogance in a tux—say what you like, he was still the only man who could save everybody when disaster landed. Whatever pleasures he seized were abrupt and without tenderness. When the intern woke up in a strange room in a negligee that wasn't hers it took a stunned moment or two to figure out how the boss's private party had ended. He didn't know the meaning of soft, but he could mimic it when he needed to, long enough to convince her that her file clerk husband needn't ever find out what happened. Quite a guy the boss. Hardly permitted himself to sleep. *Too much sleep makes a man brain-dull.* Fun, relaxation, good times, weekends and vacations, those were goods peddled to suckers to take their eyes off the ball. You had to admit that only a man that hard—devoid of scruples or sentimentality, possessing the savage instincts of a predator barely kept in check by social norms, equally adept at organizing industrial espionage, conjuring operating cash by sleight of hand, and keeping his work force in a state of fearful gratitude that they had a job at all—could keep things together in times like these. It is a tough and complicated world and feelings do not help to prop it up. None of this is about fun. None of this is about passing the time playing canasta. Fat-headed saps who want to get married and have babies, who dream of lace curtains and china table settings out of a catalogue, who care about the quality of the music coming from their radio (having gone without cigarettes for years to save up for an Atwater Kent), all those well-meaning simps would have found the floor collapsing under them a long time ago if he hadn't had the whip hand. Somehow they always knew that, right until the moment when he let them down.

finding out what it is like

Even a kid with a college degree finds himself scanning the want ads. *SALESMAN – Young and neat; must be able to furnish bond.* The trouble is he doesn't have any experience except hanging out at the track and staying up late in nightclubs. His wife left him because she was fed up with his whining. *You do nothing but complain and drink and lose your job.* Now he's finding out what it is like to start at the bottom. Tries to pawn his fraternity ring and they laugh in his face. One more weak young man disposed to feeling sorry for himself. He hardly had a chance once he started letting things slide. *Guy can't help it if he gets caught in a speakeasy raid, can he? Just my luck. A guy can't even have a good time anymore without getting into trouble.* All it takes is one moment of yielding to temptation. Trying to roll a rich drunk for his wallet. Obeying a crazy impulse to smash a jewelry store window and grab that bracelet. A dollar and a quarter would have saved him. He is green at the game. Amateurs get caught. If it is their first offense that is too bad. Far too much of that stuff going on. The judge wants to send a message to society. He had his mind made up before he even looked at you. If you are from out of state it is that much worse. Once they put the chains on, nobody on the outside will ever know what happened. Might as well have been tossed into a dungeon in some foreign country where they don't even have laws. Try to lam out and they slap on another ten years. He has nowhere to run to anyway. It was only by accident he found out about his mother. A page in a hometown paper that someone used for wrapping. She was never the same after he left home.

industrialized hells

Suffering is hidden away in the shadow country. Boys locked in attics. Women with no fixed address marched at gunpoint toward holding cells. Long rows of men shackled to benches. In so many different industrialized hells the victims go unheard. *Do you know what goes on behind those stone walls?* Anyone who makes a fuss gets worked over by uniformed brutes while the warden—a man of superficial breeding—shuts himself in his office playing violin music so he can't hear the screams. He got the job because he could be relied on to look the other way. A recaptured runaway goes straight to the hot box. More than one dies under the lash. *Mules cost forty dollars a head and convicts don't cost nothin'.* Cruelty has a grinning face. Shotguns perpetually jammed under their arms. Pausing to spit tobacco juice in the middle of some foul joke. The ones who pay their salary are of a different sort. They favor dapper tailoring and finely trimmed moustaches, savoring the thought of their own invulnerability. Politicians get kickbacks from the wardens. The wardens get payoffs from the prisoners who can afford to buy favors. Reservation officials steal land deeds and falsify death certificates. A kid who never did worse than snatch milk money from a stoop winds up on a prison farm. Deprived of any recourse until he snaps. Cracks a guard's skull. Before you know it the reform school is in flames and the rebellious kids are marching toward the gates.

the eyes of broken men

Mobs gather on unexpected corners. *Who you calling reds and hobos? We're ex-servicemen!* College students fired up by rampant crookedness abduct a gangster and string him over a pit swarming with rats until he confesses every ugly detail of his scheme to muscle in on local retailers. Runaway juveniles hurl rocks at the vigilantes raiding their encampment. *There's thousands like me—and there's more hitting the road every day.* New light comes into the eyes of broken men living in lean-tos of corrugated tin as a well-heeled agitator explains what the government is doing to them. *An evil marauding crew has turned the Constitution into a bill of sale. They're not in any offices, they don't hold any titles, they're not in the cabinet, but things happen because they want them to happen.* It is a rigged system from the get-go. People have to take things in their own hands. Pick up a rake or a wrench if that's what they've got. *We're livin' in the United States—we're free and equal—or so they tell us!* An open-hearted taxi driver doesn't need a script. Straight talk and a clenched fist will do just fine. Only by then the state troopers are already on their way to bust up the meeting, on the orders of the mayor. Or of whoever the mayor takes orders from.

sticking it to the bellyachers

The men of power take their places at the long table. The speaker of the house. The campaign chairman. The steel company president. The bankers. The stockbrokers. The newspaper publishers. The radio executives. The advertising professionals. Assembled to receive their orders. Half gloating, half wary. Eyes darting around the table to see how the rest of them are reacting. Now that the election is over the pie is to be divvied up, without regard for any pantywaist preachers. Let them stick to singing "Abide with Me" and passing the plate around. A new order starts here. The horizon will be crowded with world-class naval destroyers. Every pact and treaty and entente will be renegotiated. Round up foreign-born crooks and line them against a wall. Anybody that thinks different, fat cat or otherwise, can clear out now. Everybody needs to kick in their share. Nothing for nothing. *Never in the history of this country has there been a greater opportunity offered a strong man. Strong enough to take power into his own hands if necessary.* Radio will be under full control. Broadcasts piped into factories. Uniformed community enforcers sticking it to the bellyachers. The third degree, if it comes to that. This is going to be a door-to-door merchandising operation. Highways will carry it to all points of the compass. Convoys are on their way to every town and village in America with flags and fanfare. Spread the word. *This isn't just a Depression—this is a crisis!*

Laughing Sinners

very exclusive premises

Who wants to sit around listening to speeches? *We come for a party and all we get is some fat-headed politician listening to his own hot air.* One of the revelers turns the dial only to land on some sort of symphony. *Tie a can to that highbrow music—play something snappy.* A hot band has them jumping soon enough. The frolic is getting raucous. *I feel just like doing everything we oughtn't to do.* Dropping bottles off the balcony to watch them smash. Showgirls laugh themselves giddy. *How about a bottle of cold champagne for two little girls?* When the house detective shows up to lodge a complaint he gets a blast of seltzer in the face. If you can't do anything you want to in an artist's penthouse on New Year's Eve, with skylights and mirrors and nude paintings on the wall, then where in heck can you? *They used to arrest you for just thinking stuff like that.* These are very exclusive premises. Behind closed doors. They can't contain themselves, so why try. *I want a cocktail and I want it now.* The debauched old-timer brandishes the silver cocktail shaker like maracas, humming a silly song of his own invention with a well-practiced fatuous smile on his face. At midnight the racket of whistles and noisemakers drowns out even the saxophones.

silk crepe contours

Somewhere is a paradise of lingerie. All the underwear decked out in ads or in the backrooms of elite fashion shops is being modeled all at once in a space that goes on forever. Seductive giggles and knowing murmurs blend with the amplified glissandos of a harp ensemble. *I think I'll get a dress without any back at all. It's such beautiful silk you can almost see through it.* Alluring silk crepe contours flow out in unmarred silhouettes, accentuated by infinitely delicate lacework, luxuriant fringes of loveliness. A pink chemise offset by sheer hosiery. Figure magic made easy. Glistening peignoirs with plunging necklines. Beach pajamas flouncing free where there was no beach. Tantalizing wisps. It is a zone where men exist only as memories—*He used to like me in black—everything had to be black—nighties, underclothes, and everything.* They dissolve in laughter that is like a waterfall. Alabaster thighs double and redouble in a reflecting pool stretching out toward moonlit waters. Alone among themselves their eyes reveal inviting depths. They have nothing to hide. Someone has draped a wrap over the doorknob to block the keyhole in case some drooling wiseguy has a mind to take a peek.

old coots can't really win

The men are off by themselves knocking it back in a hotel room. – *That liquor last night was slow poison.* – *Well, I'm in no hurry.* Men with red faces, their heaving paunches almost popping out of their tuxes. Swapping lies and wheezing with laughter at their own filthy jokes while waiting for the girls to get back from the powder room. They managed to ditch their wives at the hotel, tuckered out as the women said they were after a day's shopping spree. The goggle-eyed men don't want to waste any more time but the girls keep finding ways to delay the proceedings. Always slipping out of a clinch at the crucial moment. When the geezers start to realize they've been had they talk about calling the police on them but it doesn't take long to think better of that. They have their reputations to consider. It will all surely get patched up the next night anyway—a silver bracelet in a little gift box works wonders—unless they have the bad luck to run into their wives, who meanwhile are gallivanting with the young tour guides, smoothies who were so kind as to give them their engraved cards and offer to show them the town's select night spots. Old coots can't really win. Sometime after midnight they'll be wiping their brows in chagrin and letting themselves be escorted sheepishly back to the hotel by their respective battle axes. The girls are in the powder room laughing their heads off and plotting their next moves. *Don't do anything I wouldn't do. And that covers a lot of territory.*

finely sliced baloney

The girls know it all even if knowing doesn't seem to get them very far. Never mind about that. They still have plenty of tricks up their sleeve. Whatever it takes not to wind up in a jam like the rest of the suckers. All those dames mooning over some guy that isn't worth it. *He's not the only bozo on the block.* Out in the sticks where radio is like a message from Mars it's even deadlier. *All over the country thousands of girls sitting around home in the small towns tuning in on that stuff and saying, Boy, don't they have fun in New York?* Crooners come on with their eyewash about My Blue Heaven. And the soap operas with their load of finely sliced baloney. *The Happiness Hunters—a couple of saps who are always talking about happiness and haven't got a dime.* In between the songs and the sob stories are the commercials that roll around in your head whether you want them there or not. *Use Alka-Seltzer, the favorite of so many for relief that does so much! Lifetime Oxydol washes clothes sparkling white for life! Each box of Cracker Jack comes with a free prize! Ask your dealer for Fatima in the bright sunny yellow pack! To be everlastingly beautiful use Glenelle products! At last there's a real biscuit for every dog!* It gets so bad you wake up dreaming of hair cream or mouthwash. *Marconi's gift to the morons. Cheap tripe wrapped in pretty packages for yokels.* A girl that works in broadcasting can't stand to hear any of it when she comes home. *It's hard enough listening to the radio all day on the job without getting it here too.*

they can't get arrested

Back in college when they wrapped up every dance with *Muskrat Ramble* people thought they were a hot combo. They used to have plenty of pep. Now it feels like time to look for a steady job delivering ice or something. Like the saying goes they can't get arrested. The club managers have gone cold. *Straight band acts are through. I can go to that phone and there'll be bands like yours waiting outside like a bread line.* Hitting up that kind of guy for what he owes is asking to be knocked on the head in the alley outside the dressing room. *Back pay? That's a laugh. You oughta be paying me.* The music business sure is a tough game. There has to be some way to get on the other side of those soundproofed studio windows. Once you make it in there you are at the center of the world, where all the music comes from. Nobody can even see you. You stand behind the microphone and whatever comes out of your mouth is pure magic to the chumps out in Radioland. From there on it is all gravy.

Bright Lights

the guy that made Broadway famous

Broadway is a fickle mistress people say. Broadway forgets nothing. Broadway can forgive anything if you know how to put over a song. Broadway couldn't exist without grouchy men in suits ready to back a show as long as their favorite chorine gets the featured number. *Ninety percent of sucker money is brought in by a skirt.* Broadway couldn't exist without the camaraderie of half-starved dancers showing up for auditions only to find the backers already pulled out. Broadway couldn't exist without vicious rivalry. Broadway couldn't exist without names in electric lights and stars who know how to act like stars. Who came up the hard way. *I played in every stock company from Toronto to Louisville. I've struggled for nineteen years to get where I am.* Broadway couldn't exist without the lies and thievery of press agents and promoters. Couldn't exist without stage mothers and song pluggers and bootleggers. Couldn't exist without small-town kids craving to become notorious who lie awake dreaming up nutty stunts to get their picture in the tabloids, like taking a bath in a tub full of champagne. Couldn't exist without sheer gall. *Baby, I'm the guy that made Broadway famous.* Broadway doesn't exist. It folded when the market crashed. *All the real talent went Hollywood on us.* The creditors came for the sets and costumes. Last season's hit songwriter is reduced to sleeping in the park. Wakes up to hear a bird on a branch chirping his next hit. A perfect number for the demure cutie who wangled a walk-on in the next Shubert show. That is how a factory girl from Pawtucket became the toast of 42nd Street. She throws it all away to marry a petroleum heir she met in Palm Beach. On their honeymoon they fly down to Havana for the races. By then the songwriter is in hock to gamblers and has to sign away his publishing rights on a show he hasn't written yet. Turns out it didn't really matter since it closes out of town. These days everybody is saying the same thing. *Show business in New York isn't what it used to be.*

the mouse not the message picture

Lately it seems people go to see movies about people who go to see movies. In every other feature a girl wants to be a star. Meanwhile at precisely that moment a bunch of producers are sitting around looking for the right face for their new picture. She has to be something truly unusual. By now there isn't much that folks haven't seen. *You can't put over anything anymore.* That won't stop a waitress from Battle Creek, Iowa determined to hop on the next train for Los Angeles. All the casting offices tell her there is nothing going at the studios, so she's forced to take a job modeling swimwear. How would she know the sharp-looking guy smoking a cigar on the settee is a top executive of Modern Age Productions? *The minute he meets a girl he starts feeling her ribs and talking about screen tests.* When she sees her name on the marquee it goes straight to her head. After her third picture flops she finds out how the deal works. *In this business when you're over 32 you're older than those hills out there.* They've signed your replacement before you even knew you were out of a job. By then the producers have already found their next big star only they are still in the same conference room yelling at each other—they don't know what it is like to be satisfied—trying to come up with the right vehicle for their sensational newcomer. In the movies the people who make movies never seem to have any idea what they are doing. They are always stumped for a fresh thought, drumming their fingers on the table, mopping their brows until someone—some fresh-faced Western Union messenger who's been writing plays since he was in the fourth grade—makes a golden suggestion while they are signing for the telegram. *Maybe what people really want is a little silliness.* Says it with such a heartfelt grin it comes across like pure genius. *Maybe this kid has something.* They haven't been keeping their eye on the ball, the executives have to admit it, making a bunch of serious pictures, gloomy sob stories about breadlines that are about as entertaining as a cargo manifest. What is fun after all when you come down to it? Not having to think, letting your mind pop out of its grooves. They don't want a night at the symphony, they want a day at the beach. That is why Mickey Mouse is wiping up the floor with them. People are looking for some mental relief. They come for the mouse not the message picture. They don't go to the movies to be reminded of what's going on in the world.

the blank verse of the twentieth century

He is the hottest young playwright in the country and he doesn't care who knows it. His play about mental breakdown in the trenches won all the prizes and a major studio snapped it up. Back in New York somebody who knows the score told him: If you act like an artist they'll treat you like an artist. These Hollywood types wouldn't know an intellectual concept if it bit them in the rear. *This is the land of make-believe. Everybody is makin' believe.* Now in the corner of a cocktail party he holds a small circle of listeners spellbound with his enthusiasm for the untapped cultural potential of the movies. *The photoplay is America's authentic folk drama! Why it's nothing less than modernism for the millions! Where the Bauhaus meets the Bronx! Imagism for the underdogs!* The slightly cockeyed blonde doesn't understand a word he's saying but it sounds pretty she tells him. Later he tries to explain how the patter in gangster pictures is the blank verse of the twentieth century. *It's language made aerodynamic. If Christopher Marlowe were still around he'd be writing for Warner's.*

steal it from somebody else's dream

Writers take notes while drunks spin yarns in saloons.
If a hustler makes with an entertaining line of gab in
the next barber chair they don't miss a word. They scan
the crime pages looking for a murder with some original
touches. They think nothing of reading other people's
mail. When they are stuck in a waiting room they monitor
the secretary's phone call while she tells her friend about
her night out at the Brown Derby. They flip the stories
and shuffle them, cap them and top them, turn them inside
out. You might even dream a good one, or steal it from
somebody else's dream if you catch them talking about it.
Everybody is listening in on everybody else, that is the hell
of it, all of them on the lookout for a situation or a setup
to get the juices flowing. *Will it make a movie?* Everybody
knows all the stories have been told. There have only
been 26 plots in the entire history of literature. It's all
in the telling. With the right touch a writer can still get
some action out of the most primeval hokum—a mother
sacrificing everything for kids who don't care, a daughter
going up singlehanded against the political machine to
clear her father's name—all those scripts that have been
drifting around among back-country stock companies
since Grant was president. You know what they say:
everything comes back. Crook plays about purloined land
deeds and the power of mesmerism and houses where the
lights are always going out in thunderstorms. Nobody's
done *East Lynne* in a while. Isn't it time for a new version
of *Uncle Tom's Cabin?* This is desperation and he knows

it. All he can come up with is a story about his own story: a panicky writer hungry for a new angle finds out there are no new angles. But he will keep at it until the axe falls, anything to stave off the moment when an associate producer rolls his eyes and mutters *Here we go again.* He will grab at the empty air and conjure a story out of anything at all—that altercation at the cigar counter when he was stepping into the elevator, the afternoon light hitting the stenographer as she glances moodily out the window, the pattern on the necktie of the executive sitting across the table from him—never pausing for breath or losing eye contact, grabbing hold of the ghost of a notion and twisting it into something quick, slick, and as disposable as an empty pack of chewing gum, and wangling a verbal acceptance before anybody has time to wonder what happened. So percolated he improvised a pitch and then forgot what it was all about five minutes after he sold it.

every last bit of chitchat and backtalk

There was never such a market for words. The nation is vibrating to the rhythms of talk. In headlines and comic strips and gossip columns and pulp mysteries and heartthrob romances the writers manage to find something they can use. Heard it on the street, heard it on the radio, heard it in a nightclub torch song, heard it in a dirty joke that might work with a little cleaning up, heard it at the front desk of a fleapit hotel, through the wall of the adjacent phone booth, murmured in whorehouses or muttered on the El train, screamed from the bleachers or the ringside. If they need a change of mood they can swivel the dial to pick up the distant drone of high-toned palaver from pulpits and podiums, words about social order, the advancement of civilization, the perfectibility of the race. You can never run out of material. It's out there ready to be chopped up into bite-size morsels. A phrase fit for a professor or a cabdriver or an out-of-work factory hand with his head full of Socialism or a daffy debutante back from Monte Carlo or an architect with a plan for the world's most efficient escalator. Lift a snippet from the Sunday book supplement, some gem of wisdom from George Santayana or Dale Carnegie. The so-called modern world by now is nothing but a row of typewriters ceaselessly pounding out copy, Richard Halliburton on the high road to adventure, William Beebe on the ocean floor, Will James on the lone prairie, the story of philosophy, the art of contract bridge, the latest bestselling sagas of the intimate side of life at the court of Louis the

Fifteenth or in the tobacco fields of old Virginia. From under the counter in hole-in-the-wall bookstores come secrets of dream interpretation and hypnotism and the Rosicrucian masters, marital guides for the uninformed of tender age or French imports in plain brown wrappers set in the fleshpots of ancient Carthage or the music halls of Paris—if not comics diagramming the debaucheries of Popeye the Sailor or Minnie Mouse, or personal true-life memoirs of correctional spanking. Steal a joke or two from *Judge* or *Captain Billy's Whiz Bang*, a word-painting of the Amazon or the Gobi Desert from *National Geographic*, the layouts of today's most forward-looking interior decorators from *American Home*. When it comes to words you don't have to look far: the trick would be to figure out how to get away from them, to find a locale without even a label or a title or a slogan. You have to hike pretty deep into the desert or the mountains not to look at a billboard or a discarded candy wrapper. The remotest small-town paper swarms with brain teasers and poems and inspirational filler and helpful advice about the relief of neuralgia and full-page fine-print ads that are like novelettes about socially undesirable recluses and weaklings who finally turn the table with the help of deodorant sprays or piano lessons. The print gets smaller and smaller until to read the copy they need one of those X-ray binoculars offered for sale in the back pages of the pulps. It's all research. By the time they're through they've raked over every last bit of chitchat and backtalk salvaged from a lifetime of listening. And if they haven't listened close enough they can always siphon it from someone who has. It could make your head hurt just thinking about it. If you keep tuning in all the revue sketches and burlesque skits, all the moss-covered puns and spoofs handed down from one trouper to another in the great network of small-time theatrical enterprise, and all the words gushing out of radios, the news bulletins and interviews and tear-jerking playlets, the spots for toothpaste and laxatives and sprays to kill garden pests, the ad libs barked out by announcers desperate to avoid even a half-second of dead air, all the words of all the songs, all the homers and high flies into the stands of all the ballgames, will there be anything that can possibly have been left unsaid? Will there be enough time left for even one moment of absolute unadulterated silence?

the bait

The newsstand is a wall of magazine covers. There is no end to cowboys and aviators and detectives, to girls waiting to be swept off their feet by a Royal Mountie or champion golfer, to reptilian space monsters or throned warlords with pincer-like fingernails. No end to anything in the age of paper abundance. And outshining that confusion of thrills are the faces on the covers of *Photoplay* and *Motion Picture Classic* and *Screen Book* and *Modern Screen*. The radiant floral display of sparkling eyes, luxuriant hair, gleaming teeth, pouting lips, winsome smiles. A cathedral of beauty. The cover lines promise the answer to every question: *Is Dietrich Through?—Do Movies and Marriages Mix?—What Is Success Doing To Joan Crawford?* Here is the bait that every hard-luck Hollywood extra ends up cursing as she sits alone all day in a tiny rented bungalow waiting for the phone call from Central Casting that never comes. Kids like her throw their lives away because they caught a glimpse of Karen Morley or Wallace Ford on the cover of *Screenland*. Somebody told her she was a ringer for Madge Evans. The way he lit a girl's cigarette for her, Franchot Tone couldn't have done it any better. They march without hope down Hollywood Boulevard under the big print of billboards, crushed by the unescapable language of neon signs and wall posters and marquees.

The Code

do the movies give them ideas

Some of them are reform school girls, some are boys from the work farm. They are doing time for whatever you can imagine, truancy, vagrancy, burglary, assault with intent to commit robbery, sexual delinquency. One at a time each is ushered in to talk to the man with the notebook on the other side of the table. He is only there to conduct a survey, there is no need to worry about anything. He doesn't look threatening, not a cop or a mouthpiece, more like a schoolteacher. An outsider to their world. He asks questions about what kind of life they've been living and how they ended up in this place. Then he starts in on the moving pictures. What have they seen, and how young were they when they saw it? What do they like? What do they remember? Do the movies give them ideas? Do they learn things about life? Did they ever try out any of the things they saw? Have they ever covered their eyes because of what was happening in the movie? Are they afraid of Chinese people because of movies about opium dens? Have they seen people smoking cigarettes in the movies? Did people kiss? Did they take things that weren't theirs? How did they do it? Did they climb through windows when people weren't home? Pick the pockets of drunks lying in the street? How did it feel to watch people kissing? What kind of dresses did the women wear? Were they different from the clothes that other women wore? Did the men have a lot of money? Drive expensive cars? How did it feel to look at those cars and clothes? Did they go dancing? What kind of places did they drive to? Was it late at night? Was there music playing? What kind of music? How would you describe the type of dancing that went on there? Did the men with the roadsters leave big tips? How do you think they got the money to leave the tips? What do people like that know about secure hiding places and coded messages? Do they have private slang so they can plan things without any snooper getting wise? Do they carry concealed firearms? Are they one up on everybody else? None of the "subjects" (as they are called in the notes where he classifies them by age and racial origin and economic background) will likely ever see the report about how boys and girls get stirred up by going to the pictures. Their idea of freedom is to go out and have a good time but watch your step. If a boy wants to have relations with a girl all he has to do is take her to one of those photoplays. Later on at parties they have hot times talking about the pictures they saw. This world goes too fast and you don't have time enough to think. Everything happens on the spur of the moment. A guy passes by a joint and he goes inside and gets drunk without ever planning to. His only idea is always to have plenty of money and ride around in swell machines and grab a girl whenever he wants. Be one of those that play dice and hold people up and take their money. Jimmy windows open and cut the wires on burglar alarms. Drown out gunshots by backfiring a car and other tricks like that. Any double-crosser he would take for a ride and shoot him. Be flush enough to give girls diamond bracelets and rings and fur coats. Talk like Jim Cagney. The girls love the movies. There isn't anything they haven't seen in the movies. Her mother told her movies weren't good for her but she acted like a sneak and took money from the kitchen drawer so she could go. Girls in movies go in cars to roadhouses. When she sees pictures like that she goes wild. Once the kissing starts she has a hot feeling going through her and wants to do everything bad. She craves nothing but love and wild parties. At parties she met the men that were crazy for fast life. The future? She is spending her days until her time is up thinking of how to make money while she is young, faster than you can make it in a factory or a dentist's office. She's seen it done all kind of ways.

to be warriors

The monsignor submits his rough draft to the committee:

This is a call to the youth of America. If you care about staying strong and healthy, if you care about living up to the hopes of those who love you most, you will want to join the struggle for a cleaner nation. The merchants of pollution have targeted you. You are the ones they want to corrupt—yes, even though you have never dreamt of such a thing, they have marked you as the next victim of their scheme to turn every young American into a dedicated patron of spectacles of degradation. The Roman Empire fell when it debased human virtue for the applause of an intoxicated rabble. The great nations of Europe sank into decline when they allowed the most vicious practices to become common pastimes of an enervated elite, an elite only too eager to consort with the lowest merchants of filth and immoral servitude. And such merchants are with us today. No mere ocean barrier could keep them out. They have used every trick of gaudy display and cheapjack finery to elevate the muck of depraved exploitation into a veneer of respectable entertainment, inviting the public and most especially you—the young spectators who hold the promise of the future!—into those emporia with their sweets and soft drinks and velvety seats, with their dim lights encouraging the stolen kiss and the furtive caress, where they spread out their enticing and poisonous wares. It's not only your money they want, those hard-earned coins that you have been persuaded to plunk down to lay eyes on the latest bare-shouldered beauty or the latest piece of sophisticated immodesty cooked up by Broadway cynics who have drunk the wine of mockery— it isn't only your money, as dearly as they want that, but so much more—your bodies, your minds, your very souls. Is it not the voice of the tempter you hear in those sonorous fanfares that announce their newest unveiling of tantalizing promises, in those entrancing flirtations issuing from the lips of a nightclub dancer or woman of pleasure as she beckons you into that bower of self-gratification that is in truth as bitter in its aftertaste as the ashes of Sheol?

I do not mean to denigrate the movies. We have all loved the movies. The movies represent perhaps the unlooked for and incomparable flowering of our technical civilization. What great delight we have taken in the natural wonders and feats of skill that we have witnessed—the pinnacles of art and architecture that we have been able to explore as if we were there ourselves—mighty dams and other triumphs of engineering—the inspiring visualization of glorious episodes from literature and history and scripture itself. We have laughed at the fun of good-natured clowns. We have thrilled at heroes on horseback riding to the rescue of innocence in distress. We have been moved by the depiction of great human stories told with sincerity and high dramatic art. The movies are our heritage. At their best they can be a vehicle for the finest human thoughts and aspirations. But that heritage is at risk. You don't want to believe it, but it is so. The men who undertake to appropriate it do not care a fig for noble thoughts or immortal aspirations. They serve the golden calf, not the commandments handed down on Sinai. They serve it as only those can who are so steeped in degeneracy that their eyes are blinded to all that is fine and their ears deaf to all that cries out for pity and succor. The spawn of cramped and foreign cities, where human life is worth no more than the handful of coins for which it is routinely exchanged, they are not the ones who will lift up their eyes to the far hills or heed the inner voice that ordains decorum and reverence. If they offer you, in your place of relaxation, images of the harlot and the gangster, the narcotic addict and the adulteress and the cheap and whiskey-addled newspaperman who would sell his soul for a headline story—if they show you women stripped naked for the perverted enjoyment of slavering strangers, and men reduced to the lowest levels of brutal aggression and feckless self-indulgence—it is because they are not capable of imagining any higher human destiny. They want to drag you down into the miasma where they themselves dwell. In vain would you turn to them for charity, or forbearance, or respect for the tender near-angelic grace of the as yet unformed child, or, indeed, respect for anything but the demands of a rapacious greed, a devouring hunger for the very marrow of the human spirit. Shall we allow this? Shall we let them buy us for a mess of celluloid pottage, a handful of false flickering dreams? Surely we are made of better stuff than to let what is most precious fall into the hands of street peddlers and heartless traffickers. We are called upon to build a culture—to build a world—that embodies the best that we are and may become. We are called—and you in particular, my young friends, as is ever the burden and challenge of youth, are called—to be warriors. Fight the filthy films. Let us have clean art in a clean America. Join the legion. Join the boycott.

one picture one plotline one audience

The head of production sends out a memo:

There's been a lot of talk about the recent changes in the industry because of the enforcement of the Production Code. I don't want to discuss anybody's objections to what the Code spells out because frankly that train has left the station. What I want to talk about is what's wrong with our pictures and the fact that we may now have a golden opportunity to make them better. Our pictures haven't been delivering because they aren't giving the public what it wants, the whole public, not a specialty crowd. Our pictures are threadbare. Ho-hum. Flat as last night's beer. Walk into a movie theater and what do you see? A worn-out hooker watching the rain fall out the window of a broken-down hotel. A young guy whining about how he can't find a job. Or maybe a couple of stuffed-shirt butler types standing around like statues in what was supposed to be Broadway's bright new hit except they forgot to tell the audience. People don't want to go the movies to see the same stuff they could see looking out the window. And they don't want to see actors who look like they came straight out of the icebox speaking English like they've got a broom up their rear end. Audiences want to be lifted out of themselves. They want to be surprised. They want to feel good about the future. And we can make that happen. We have the talent and the skills and the equipment but we haven't been getting one-tenth of the juice we could out of them.

Our writers come up with some good lines, they ought to for what we pay them, but when you see the picture the lines are thrown away. Half the audience doesn't get it, doesn't even hear it. Did anybody care? Did the writers care? Did the director care? We make them feel dumb when we ought to be making them feel like they're on top of the world. We confuse them with words and names they've never heard in their lives, and people who talk too fast, or foreign accents where they can hardly make out a word. We give them risqué witticisms and they're embarrassed because they don't understand the point, and then resentful because they figure we're trying to embarrass them. From here on in we've got to set up situations and scenes and characters so that every line hits home. Everybody laughs or cries at the same time. Anybody that doesn't feel like laughing or crying, they're free to react any way they please, but I assure you they will be in a minority and we don't make pictures for minorities. Everybody in the audience should know what he's feeling, know who he's rooting for. I don't want anybody sitting in a movie house wondering what the hell is going on, who's supposed to be the hero, what kind of a picture is this, is this supposed to be a comedy or a tragedy or some kind of informational program. Some people may grouse about the new restrictions on sex stories, salty language, and the like, but we can bring in customers who stayed away because of the sensational stuff. It may come as news to you, but for most of the ticket-buying public

New York isn't the center of the world, it's a temporary aberration. And they never heard of George Bernard Shaw or Gertrude Stein either. Don't worry about the old customers, they're not going anywhere. They like movies too, and they'll stick around because there's nowhere else to go. From now on every picture we make is for everybody, everywhere. One picture, one plotline, one audience. Save the sex stories and the salty language for your private amusement, I know that won't be a problem for any of you—and while you're at it save the German camera angles and the James Joyce literary references and the allegorical dream sequences—and let's all get back into the business of making great and profitable motion pictures.

After Tomorrow

people I met in a dream

Finally I had to admit I'd never get anywhere in Hollywood. You keep a dream alive until the morning it goes sour on you. I'd been beating the pavement for days, plain out of luck in a city where luck is almost everything. Nothing but the last of some money from home to tide me over until I climbed on board the bus that would take me away from everything I thought was worth getting to in the first place. When I ducked into the beat-looking tavern on the corner it was because I'd run out of places to park myself. It promised nothing, but it was full of people. More than I imagined could fit in such a hole in the wall, lining the bar, clustered around shadowy tables, swarming, arguing, yelling for what looked like the fun of it. Somebody was playing *Goofus* on the out-of-tune piano. They all talked at the same time, the shrieks and growls sloshing around like an aquarium tank for slightly used humans. How could they be so old. A miracle any survived to stretch a hand across the bar for one more slug. Pickled in alcohol for a hundred years. None seemed quite normal but then who is. Nothing more ordinary than being damn peculiar. Who doesn't know some character forever holed up in his room, a geezer who once a year on the anniversary of the Battle of Manila Bay dresses in Spanish-American War gear. Or a widow who spouts verses from the Lamentations of Jeremiah and forecasts hellfire for young people who dance the shimmy. Floozies gone goofy with years of too much drink. Boxers with half their brains knocked out. Extravagant artistic types who sing Rossini arias off key and throw champagne bottles at barroom mirrors when the devil is in them. All the odd ones drifted in here. It was a reunion of people I met in a dream. A little splotchier, more coarse-grained and scarred, drained of the last trace of youth. They wore their hair differently once. Sported pearls or tiepins they probably had to hock. Faces I had seen only for a few seconds, but where? Milling among top-hatted swells at a concert, filling the lobby with a rumbling approximation of intelligent chatter? Standing on line with panicky depositors, waiting to get their money out before the bank went bust? Reveling on New Year's Eve with toy horns and funny hats? This one, loosening his collar after the last round, resembled an English valet seriously letting his hair down on his day off. Another could pass for a live version of the coin-operated Gypsy Fortune Teller at Ocean Park. Faces came into focus one by one, superimposed on the faces at the bar the way they do for ghost scenes in the movies. Somebody's dowager aunt. A Follies girl left in the lurch. A kid fresh out of high school staring at the counter of the soda shop like his best girl stood him up and he doesn't know where to take it from there. A nerve case who must be some kind of henchman or stool pigeon, most likely a hophead, constantly checking over his shoulder to see if he's being tailed... Had I been looking for a place like this all my life?

A foaming glass of beer slid across the counter. *Here, take the head off this.* A weight I never knew was there was lifted. *We're just sittin' around gassin'.* The atmosphere around me felt jumpy and loose at the same time. *It's a free country, isn't it?* Talking loud and keeping their eyes open. Not taking any guff off anybody. Everybody a wisecracker. *Don't take it personal. Everybody has to let off steam sometime. If you can't take a ribbing better steer clear.* They started in on their private histories of show business.—*Those cheap hotels and their lobby comics?—You said it, sister. Rotten beds, greasy grub, lonely as an alley cat.* The small-town deputies looking for a payoff in one currency or another, the stage door mashers and cornfed Romeos, the lecherous drummers trying their luck after showing off their line of corsets, the snooping landladies. Theatrical boarding houses where they slept six to a room and fought over table scraps. Jumping out a bedroom window a few yards ahead of a jealous husband with a shotgun. Waking before sunup to catch the train to Omaha. And missing it. Or getting there to find the costumes already repossessed by creditors. *Cooking our own food, washing our own clothes and ironing them—on mirrors—going ragged all summer and then damn near freezing in the winter.* Histories of flubbed lines and drunken entrances and costumes ripping at the worst possible moment. The greasepaint that never quite comes all the way off. The story of how they got cheated out of the role of a lifetime by the stage manager's hateful bedmate. The story of how they got unceremoniously groped by the finest classical actor of our time. The story of how they lost all their money. *I sweat a century in every rat-trap theater in America and a lot of half-witted brokers throw my earnings in the nearest sewer!* And then there was the story of how the world looked before the money went away. *I was out of the chorus line riding in my own carriage long before they knew whether* Florodora *was going to be a hit or a flop.*

It didn't matter if anyone believed it, or if they believed it themselves. It was nothing but an act anyway, on either side of the swinging doors. *We're all just playing a part, kid, only some of us know it.* He was just warming up, he'd been warming up all his life. *It helps to know what you're doing, especially if you're play-acting. No one better for a duchess than a whore, or to peddle God like the snake-oil man. Set a thief to play a copper.* I looked into the face of the oldtimer—or at least he'd been playing old men since he was twelve, and living on the road since he was eight— and thought I detected wisdom behind the rheumy eyes. Sat there waiting to be initiated into mysteries as he went on with his story whose beginning was forgotten but which turned out to be the same story he had already told when I started listening. *And what do you think I said then? I'll give you one good guess. You should have seen the look on the guy's face. You had to be there.* He wasn't as far gone as he seemed and knew exactly when I started tuning out. He stared through me. *A young fella like you, you have no idea what I'm talking about, do you? You'll learn soon enough. Mind you watch out for those four-in-the-morning dialogues with the dead. You can't ever win those kinds of arguments. Dead or as good as. Leastways you aren't going to see them again, unless they was in the movies some time.*

how much they could leave out

More and more these days it is like waking in a white and empty space. The walls left unpainted too long, and nobody thought to put up any kind of ornament or picture. As if somebody made a bet to see how much they could leave out without getting a complaint. Clean, in its gashed and worn-down way. Or more like cleaned out. Daylight lays the seams and joints bare. Nail marks and cracks where the wood splintered. There are gaps all over the place, where things eroded or got gouged off. Being broke does that even to comfortable homes like this must have been. The wind gets in and that is it. On the little side table by the bed with the broken springs a postcard from a town in another part of the country. A message in an old woman's scrawl to say she hopes things work out. This room is not made for words. It is a place for being out of place. You are getting used to having nowhere to go, no plan beyond the next lift or handout or temporary meal ticket. Looking at a big future as a professional scrounger. At the far edge of where you managed to get to you end up where you have been living all along without knowing it. No credit line and not a thing to hang on to or leave behind. That kind of wipes the chalk off the board. Being alone means having plenty of company. Walk outside and it looks like everybody joined the same club. The money drained away and even the world-famous retail emporiums look fake and weightless. Cities are their own skeletons. If there are stories they are about there no longer being anything to tell stories about, and what people do after that happens. A lot of bare and hungry hours are being stored up for a time you can't see your way toward just now. When someone eventually comes around looking for second-hand memories, for traces and scraps of forgotten talk, they will probably be expecting something different. Of this chill morning light, anyway, they will find nothing.

ALOYSIUS AT 18

I was heading out the exit not even seeing the street,
still keyed up, hanging on to that bounce, and already
feeling it slip away. Happens every time after a picture
or a show if they're any good. Didn't want to miss the
chance to catch *Duck Soup* again. In the light of Eighth
Avenue I'm still running through the jokes, trying to
nail the words so I can play them back in my head for a
lift. Rehearsing Groucho's song, Rufus T. Firefly laying
down the laws of his administration: *You're not allowed
to smoke... Or tell a dirty joke... And whistling is
forbidden.* Not a bad description of parochial school.
Nothing has been funnier than *Duck Soup* as far as I
can recall. *Will you marry me? Did he leave you any
money? Answer the second question first.* How often does it
happen that everything clicks, no clunkers, no dead
spots? Most shows let you down. They start great but
peter out. The last act has nowhere to go. There are
reasons why *Duck Soup* is the funniest of all movies. I
could make a list. Because it has the nerve not to fall
for any kind of baloney. Never goes gooey even for a
second. Never weakens. Knows when enough is
enough. There is a line you have to keep your eye on.
It's easy not to reach it and it's easy to step over it,
damn hard to hit the point. Keep a straight face. Show
no pity. Keep one step ahead of everybody. Push it as
far it goes and then move on fast. Like Groucho or
Durante or Cagney. No fooling around with them. The
timing, the attitude. How to slip off an overcoat or
light up a smoke. Nothing cluttered, nothing muffled.
They all try but so few can do it. I think I can. That
murder mystery last week—the family gathered for the

reading of the will, the lights going out, the corpse on the living room floor—the whole cast was from hunger. Petrified acting. I could do any of those bits better. Rackets boss snarling, milquetoast desk clerk hemming and hawing, shell-shocked soldier falling apart in the trenches, slinking henchman, senator from Dixie oozing molasses, silly ass houseguest who gets all the laughs. But nothing is real without an audience. I have no place to use what I've got. Wondering where to go next, walking down Broadway feeling like a character in a play, looking at the marquees, keeping an eye out for the snazzy dames you see around here, taking a gander at what Lunt and Fontanne and Katharine Cornell and the Theatre Guild are up to. So many shows to see if I had the jack. Instead of reading what Brooks Atkinson and George Jean Nathan have to say about them while I work the pharmacy job. Never expected to be stuck in that dead end. Living with Mom and chipping in half what I make toward the rent. Dead ends all over. The New Deal has been pretty much hot air up where we live. Parades and speeches but nothing you can take to the bank. They say everybody loves a parade but I guess I'm the exception. The banks are still closed anyway. Reading the want ads and sending in letters to everything that sounds like an opening. You seem like a bright kid they say before putting me on the wait list. Just hear me out. I can tell a joke and think on my feet. You want to talk ball games? Prize fighters? Russ Columbo? The situation in Europe? Labor unions? The future of the Republican Party? Amelia Earhart? Noël Coward?

H. V. Kaltenborn? I could go on and on. All that fine
talk spilling into the night and going nowhere. There's
a hundred things I could be doing. Depression or no
Depression, the town is awash in talent contests and
theatrical agents. Hollywood people looking for new
faces. I'm ready to go up against the other young
operators on the make. So many they bump into each
other on the sidewalk, salesmen running their spiels in
every doorway, actors practicing how to sell hair cream
over the airwaves. I'm learning the language of sports
reporters, fight promoters, radio announcers and
emcees. You have to know this stuff to hold your head
up. If you don't want to end like the beaten-down ones
that never made the cut or even tried. You don't have
to invent the lightbulb or discover the Oregon Trail,
but these guys barely got off the block where they
were born. When I look at what they do to themselves,
with booze or just being too much alone. On benches
or in bars or single-occupancy rooms. There are so
many ways to lose. A guy can finish school and raise a
family and get stuck in a job that hardly pays the bills
but he's scared to ask for a raise. People end up kidding
themselves, piping up on cue with the same lines, the
same line readings. They're in a play and they don't
know it. Most of what they say comes from somebody
else who didn't know what they were talking about
either. It gets passed along from one megaphone to
another until it sounds like it must mean something.
Mouthing the words like the Latin mass. People bow
their heads on Sundays as if they were paying
attention when they don't understand a word. It

sounds familiar, it's comforting. You want to grab them
and tell them to snap out of their trance. Didn't you
make the same remark yesterday and every day of your
life? Like a school lesson that keeps repeating. Show
some respect why don't you. Don't use such language.
Don't catch a cold. It just goes to show. Show what?
They'll do it every time, in the immortal words of
Jimmy Hatlo. They are nice people of course. They
mean well but don't know enough not to set wet shoes
to dry by a radiator. Trusting souls. Easy marks who
wouldn't dream of making a scene. A charming
stranger who uses words of more than three syllables
could con them out of their life's savings. The
harmless people. And then there are the real
knuckleheads, the ones who aren't interested in
anything at all. Not a book or an oil painting or even a
tomato with class. It's all the same to them. If they
saw *Aida* at the Met, with that Verdi music sweeping
out from the pit and Martinelli singing Radamès, they
wouldn't know what to do with it. Would rather hear
Rudy Vallée doing the Stein Song. Don't mind every
day being pretty much the same as the one that just
happened, and on top of that don't mind punching out
anybody that says different. Not a thought in their
head. The whole country seems to be swarming with
them. Like the mob of morons that lynched those
kidnappers in San Jose last November. Two drifters
who killed the poor sonofabitch they were holding for
ransom. But all the same. Supposedly there were ten
thousand in that lynch mob, storming the jail and
hanging the guys in a public park, with the governor

of the state egging them on in the name of law and
order. The same kind of goons who keep Tom Mooney
locked up for something he didn't do. The money
interests will never cut a working man a break. It
could tear your heart out if you let it get to you, the
way the dummies end up running things. They can't
get enough of themselves. Archbishops, teachers,
politicians, finaglers all the way down the line. The
ancient Egyptians had rackets like Tammany Hall.
And they start believing their own publicity. On
Washington's birthday a stooge in a high hat quotes
Emerson on self-reliance as if he ever opened a book in
his life. The priests herd everybody into line the way
religions like to do, with their catechism and their
sermons on purity. Meantime it's up to the kids to
spread the word about not getting alone with Father
Dugan. Best part of church was the music. Fauré's
Requiem, there was a wonderful thing. The trouble
started with the words. But it's like that all over, the
rules and rituals they put you through from the first
grade on, the pledges and drills. Just to make sure
nobody has a minute to think. Or even try to have a
halfway good time. Like Groucho's song: *If any form of
pleasure is exhibited... Report to me and it will be
prohibited... I'll put my foot down, so shall it be... This is
the land of the free.* It takes an awful lot of effort to
resist the malarkey. Bold thinkers have their heads
handed to them. Galileo or Voltaire or Robert
Ingersoll. Nobody believed Heinrich Schliemann when
he started searching for the ruins of Troy. *The
Marriage of Figaro* was a flop opening night. And

Mozart was dead by the time he was thirty-five. He
had the last laugh because his music is still around.
And he had the fun of making it in the first place.
What could be better than to invent something from
scratch. O. Henry or Ring Lardner writing a story.
Heywood Broun or Franklin P. Adams sitting at the
typewriter and coming up with the words in
tomorrow's paper. That's real freedom. The audience
can sit back and let it wash over them but there's more
pleasure for the ones that do the cooking than the ones
that do the looking. Like actually being a live wire. The
best of them practice until their reflexes are second
nature. Come out strong on the first line and still leave
room to bring it up higher, slow it down when they
need to, stop it completely and let it hang there for a
moment that is like forever. They make silence work
for them. They make doing nothing work for them.
They don't laugh at their own jokes. Being a straight
man is the hardest. Dying is easy, comedy is hard. First
acts are easy, second acts are hard. Be tough. Leave
them hungry. When they say they want more they
don't. When you're really into it you can turn
everything upside down until it's hilarious. Say
something inane in a resonant voice like Westbrook
Van Voorhis on *The March of Time.* Turn all those
voices into jokes, the radio announcer with perfectly
modulated delivery pitching a deodorant or
introducing a half-hour program of ballroom music in
hushed tones. *And now, Don Bestor and His Orchestra
asking the musical question "Why?"* Outraged senators
demanding a fair deal for the farmers they rob blind.

The bishop of Cleveland shouting "Purify Hollywood
or destroy Hollywood!" People who take themselves
seriously are the funniest thing going. In Philadelphia
the church wants to boycott the movies. All the movies,
even Jeanette MacDonald and Rin Tin Tin. Everybody
should have a hobby. I saw the pledge the Legion of
Decency is handing out in the parishes. Mom brought
it home. It was good for a laugh at least. "I condemn
absolutely those salacious motion pictures which, with
other degrading agencies, are corrupting public morals
and promoting a sex mania in our land." We should be
so lucky. As far as I can see the worst thing they're
doing is bringing back a lot of hokey plays that should
never have escaped from summer stock. Anyway, would
you want to see a movie that came recommended by
the bishop of Cleveland? Take Mae West any day.
They're worried about the country falling apart and it
already did, and it wasn't the movies that did it. Where
I live the Wall Street types are as popular as Typhoid
Mary. Maybe Roosevelt will put them on a leash. And
maybe the bishops will shut down the movies, the
mayor will shut down the burlesque houses, and over
in Germany they will keep burning books. I saw the
newsreels. Nobody knows where any of this is going.
The ancient civilizations had no idea what hit them.
Most of the plays of Aeschylus and Sophocles are lost.
The survivors got through by dumb luck. The
Etruscans had a written language that nobody knows
how to read. Who knows what else got buried. The
Inca were doing all right until the Spaniards showed
up. Everybody walks on thin ice whether they know it

or not. Eat drink and be merry for tomorrow we die. *Glücklich ist, wer vergißt, was doch nicht zu ändern ist.* Happy the man who forgets what he cannot change. Johann Strauss. *Die Fledermaus.* Now there is something absolutely wonderful with no purpose at all but to make people happy. What else do you need. My father never had time to really enjoy himself. The odds were stacked. The world could be a more pleasant place but it probably won't be. According to H. G. Wells the Great War began nothing and settled nothing. Wells could make you believe we have a chance. If there were more like him. H. G. Wells for Secretary of State and Groucho for President, how about that. And a fair break for union labor. Instead you get clunks like Hitler in Germany who just organized a massacre of top politicians. First thing I saw this morning, on the front page of the *News.* HITLER FORCES SLAY 11 LEADERS OF OPPOSITION. MANY OTHERS DIE. They aren't kidding around over there. Those are the people who *really* aren't interested in anything, wouldn't know how to enjoy anything even if they had the chance. That's how bad it can get. There are always some people who hope it will. We've got them here too. Avoid becoming a character in somebody else's storyline. Free to come, free to go, free to laugh. *You can leave in a taxi. If you can't get a taxi, you can leave in a huff. If that's too soon, you can leave in a minute and a huff. If you run out of gas, get ethyl. If Ethel runs out, get Mabel...*

DOROTHY AFTER
THE SHOW

East Main Street, Nanticoke, Pa.

and walking back into the street now it's over
the movie people are already fading into wispy halos
to become part of the street and the air
it is tantalizing to have been among them
and to feel how they go away
showing how they were never here
there was a face   the picture changes   the face is gone
I'm one of them   I will be one of them
to be one of them is to be real and not fade
I know they will come back   parts of them
in broken order   after I get home
at night when I close my eyes I see pictures
some I go looking for   others come after me
the gray bodies are still wandering around
so close I could crawl in among them
they are the movies no one but me will ever see
the shadows of what no one will ever inherit
on the other side of

Appendix:
Some Pre-Code Movies

Arabian Nights of 1934 is drawn in large part from American films made between the advent of sound in the late 1920s and the full enforcement of the Production Code, which went into effect in the summer of 1934. Storylines, situations, images, and lines of dialogue are freely recombined in the book's episodes. That said, this is a fantasia rather than a work of history.

I am indebted to many writers and scholars and to all those who have worked to restore and make available the films of the pre-Code era. Among contemporaries I am particularly grateful to David Bordwell, Donald Crafton, James Curtis, Thomas Doherty, Philippe Garnier, Molly Haskell, Liz Helfgott, Kent Jones, Mick LaSalle, Patrick McGilligan, Imogen Sara Smith, Margaret Talbot, Mark A. Viera, and Victoria Wilson, as well as the late Radley Metzger. The retrospectives mounted by Bruce Goldstein at New York's Film Forum were of major importance. This book originated in notes made during a residency at the American Academy in Berlin, whose support is deeply appreciated. My interest in films of the early 30s was sparked by my aunt LaVerne Owens, who took me to see *Gold Diggers of 1933* and *42nd Street* at a propitious moment, and with whom I enjoyed conversations on the subject over many decades. My parents, Margaret and Joseph O'Brien, were constantly in my thoughts during the writing of this book. Imagining the inner monologues of their astral surrogates, Dorothy and Aloysius, has been a way of participating, at a distance, in the era in which they came of age.

The following films, whether or not directly quoted or otherwise specifically alluded to in the text, have been part of the mix.

Ace of Aces (1933). Director: J. Walter Ruben. Cast: Richard Dix, Elizabeth Allan, Ralph Bellamy.

Advice to the Lovelorn (1933). D: Alfred Werker. C: Lee Tracy, Sally Blane, Sterling Holloway.

Afraid to Talk (1932). D: Edward L. Cahn. C: Eric Linden, Sidney Fox, Louis Calhern.

After Tomorrow (1932). D: Frank Borzage. C: Charles Farrell, Marian Nixon, Minna Gombell.

The Age of Consent (1932). D: Gregory La Cava. C: Dorothy Wilson, Arline Judge, Richard Cromwell.

Air Mail (1932). D: John Ford. C: Pat O'Brien, Ralph Bellamy, Gloria Stuart, Lilian Bond.

American Madness (1932). D: Frank Capra. C: Walter Huston, Pat O'Brien, Constance Cummings.

An American Tragedy (1931). D: Josef von Sternberg. C: Phillips Holmes, Sylvia Sidney, Frances Dee, Irving Pichel.

The Animal Kingdom (1932). D: Edward H. Griffith. C: Ann Harding, Leslie Howard, Myrna Loy, Neil Hamilton, Ilka Chase.

Applause (1929). D: Rouben Mamoulian. C: Helen Morgan, Joan Peers.

Are You Listening? (1932). D: Harry Beaumont. C: William Haines, Madge Evans, Anita Page.

Baby Face (1933). D: Alfred E. Green. C: Barbara Stanwyck, George Brent, Donald Cook, Theresa Harris, Margaret Lindsay, John Wayne, Douglass Dumbrille.

Back Street (1932). D: John Stahl. C: Irene Dunne, John Boles, ZaSu Pitts.

Bad Girl (1931). D: Frank Borzage. C: James Dunn, Sally Eilers, Minna Gombell.

The Beast of Borneo (1931). D: George Melford. C: Rose Hobart, Charles Bickford, Georges Renavent.

The Beast of the City (1932). D: Charles Brabin. C: Walter Huston, Jean Harlow, Wallace Ford, Jean Hersholt.

Behind Office Doors (1931). D: Melville Brown. C: Mary Astor, Robert Ames, Ricardo Cortez.

Behind the Mask (1932). D: John Francis Dillon. C: Jack Holt, Constance Cummings, Boris Karloff, Edward Van Sloan.

Big City Blues (1932). D: Mervyn LeRoy. C: Joan Blondell, Eric Linden, Humphrey Bogart.

The Big House (1930). D: George Hill. C: Wallace Beery, Chester Morris, Robert Montgomery, Lewis Stone, Leila Hyams.

The Big Shakedown (1934). D: John Francis Dillon. C: Bette Davis, Ricardo Cortez, Glenda Farrell, Charles Farrell, Allen Jenkins.

The Black Camel (1931). D: Hamilton MacFadden. C: Warner Oland, Sally Eilers, Bela Lugosi, Robert Young.

Black Moon (1934). D: Roy William Neill. C: Jack Holt, Fay Wray, Clarence Muse, Dorothy Burgess.

Blessed Event (1932). D: Roy Del Ruth. C: Lee Tracy, Mary Brian, Dick Powell, Ruth Donnelly, Allen Jenkins.

Blonde Crazy (1931). D: Roy Del Ruth. C: James Cagney, Joan Blondell, Louis Calhern, Ray Milland, Guy Kibbee.

Blonde Venus (1932). D: Josef von Sternberg. C: Marlene Dietrich, Herbert Marshall, Cary Grant, Dickie Moore.

Blondie Johnson (1933). D: Ray Enright. C: Joan Blondell, Chester Morris, Claire Dodd.

Brief Moment (1933). D: David Burton. C: Carole Lombard, Gene Raymond, Monroe Owsley.

Blood Money (1933). D: Rowland Brown. C: George Bancroft, Frances Dee, Judith Anderson, Blossom Seeley.

Born To Be Bad (1934). D: Lowell Sherman. C: Loretta Young, Cary Grant.

The Bowery (1933). D: Raoul Walsh. C: Wallace Beery, George Raft, Fay Wray.

Broadway Thru a Keyhole (1933). D: Lowell Sherman. C: Constance Cummings, Paul Kelly, Russ Columbo, Texas Guinan, Blossom Seeley, Gregory Ratoff.

The Broadway Melody (1929). D: Harry Beaumont. C: Bessie Love, Anita Page, Charles King.

The Cabin in the Cotton (1932). D: Michael Curtiz. C: Richard Barthelmess, Bette Davis.

Call Her Savage (1932). D: John Francis Dillon. C: Clara Bow, Gilbert Roland, Thelma Todd.

Central Airport (1933). D: William Wellman. C: Richard Barthelmess, Sally Eilers.

Chance at Heaven (1933). D: William Seiter. C: Joel McCrea, Ginger Rogers, Marian Nixon.

Chandu the Magician (1932). D: William Cameron Menzies & Marcel Varnel. C: Edmund Lowe, Bela Lugosi, Irene Ware.

The Crash (1932). D: William Dieterle. C: George Brent, Ruth Chatterton.

The Circus Queen Murder (1933). D: Roy William Neill. C: Adolphe Menjou, Greta Nissen, Donald Cook, Dwight Frye.

City Girl (1930). D: F. W. Murnau. C: Charles Farrell, Mary Duncan.

Christopher Strong (1933). D: Dorothy Arzner. C: Katharine Hepburn, Colin Clive, Billie Burke, Helen Chandler.

The Criminal Code (1930). D: Howard Hawks. C: Walter Huston, Phillips Holmes, Constance Cummings, Boris Karloff.

Crooner (1932). D: Lloyd Bacon. C: David Manners, Ann Dvorak, J. Carrol Naish, Ken Murray, Claire Dodd.

Dark Hazard (1934). D: Alfred E. Green. C: Edward G. Robinson, Genevieve Tobin, Glenda Farrell.

Day of Reckoning (1933). D: Charles Brabin. C: Richard Dix, Madge Evans, Conway Tearle, Una Merkel, Stu Erwin, Spanky McFarland.

Desirable (1934). D: Archie Mayo. C: Jean Muir, George Brent, Verree Teasdale, Theresa Harris.

Dinner at Eight (1933). D: George Cukor. C: Marie Dressler, John Barrymore, Jean Harlow, Lionel Barrymore, Billie Burke, Wallace Beery, Lee Tracy.

Dishonored (1931). D: Josef von Sternberg. C: Marlene Dietrich, Victor McLaglen, Warner Oland, Gustav von Seyffertitz.

The Divorcee (1930). D: Robert Z. Leonard. C: Norma Shearer, Chester Morris, Conrad Nagel, Robert Montgomery, Florence Eldridge.

Doctor X (1932). D: Michel Curtiz. C: Lionel Atwill, Fay Wray, Lee Tracy, Preston Foster.

The Doorway to Hell (1930). D: Archie Mayo. C: Lew Ayres, Dorothy Matthews, James Cagney.

Dr. Monica (1934). D: William Keighley. C: Kay Francis, Warren William, Jean Muir.

Duck Soup (1933). D: Leo McCarey. C: The Marx Brothers, Margaret Dumont, Louis Calhern, Raquel Torres.

The Emperor Jones (1933). D: Dudley Murphy. C: Paul Robeson, Dudley Digges, Fredi Washington, Jackie "Moms" Mabley.

Employees' Entrance (1933). D: Roy Del Ruth. C: Warren William, Loretta Young, Wallace Ford, Alice White, Ruth Donnelly.

Ex-Lady (1933). D: Robert Florey. C: Bette Davis, Gene Raymond, Claire Dodd, Monroe Owsley, Ferdinand Gottschalk.

The Famous Ferguson Case (1932). D: Lloyd Bacon. C: Joan Blondell, Grant Mitchell, Vivienne Osborne.

Female (1933). D: Michael Curtiz. C: Ruth Chatterton, George Brent, Lois Wilson, Johnny Mack Brown.

The Final Edition (1932). D: Howard Higgin. C: Pat O'Brien, Mae Clarke, Bradley Page.

Finishing School (1934). D: Wanda Tuchok & George Nichols Jr. C: Frances Dee, Bruce Cabot, Ginger Rogers, Billie Burke, Theresa Harris.

Five and Ten (1931). D: Robert Z. Leonard. C: Marion Davies, Leslie Howard, Irene Rich, Richard Bennett.

Five Star Final (1931). D: Mervyn LeRoy. C: Edward G. Robinson, H. B. Warner, Marian Marsh, Aline MacMahon, Boris Karloff.

Footlight Parade (1933). D: Lloyd Bacon. C: James Cagney, Joan Blondell, Ruby Keeler, Dick Powell, Frank McHugh, Ruth Donnelly, Guy Kibbee, Hugh Herbert.

Forbidden (1932). D: Frank Capra. C: Barbara Stanwyck, Adolphe Menjou, Ralph Bellamy.

42nd Street (1933). D: Lloyd Bacon. C: Warner Baxter, Ruby Keeler, Bebe Daniels, George Brent, Dick Powell, Ginger Rogers, Una Merkel, Ned Sparks.

A Free Soul (1931). D: Clarence Brown. C: Norma Shearer, Lionel Barrymore, Clark Gable, Leslie Howard.

Frisco Jenny (1932). D: William Wellman. C: Ruth Chatterton, Louis Calhern, Donald Cook.

From Headquarters (1933). D: William Dieterle. C: George Brent, Margaret Lindsay, Eugene Pallette.

Gabriel Over the White House (1933). D: Gregory La Cava. C: Walter Huston, Karen Morley, Franchot Tone, Dickie Moore.

Going Hollywood (1933). D: Raoul Walsh. C: Bing Crosby, Marion Davies, Fifi D'Orsay.

Gold Diggers of 1933 (1933). D: Mervyn LeRoy. C: Joan Blondell, Ruby Keeler, Aline MacMahon, Dick Powell, Warren William, Ginger Rogers, Guy Kibbee.

Grand Hotel (1932). D: Edmund Goulding. C: Greta Garbo, John Barrymore, Lionel Barrymore, Joan Crawford, Wallace Beery, Lewis Stone, Jean Hersholt.

Grand Slam (1933). D: William Dieterle. C: Paul Lukas, Loretta Young, Frank McHugh, Glenda Farrell, Roscoe Karns.

The Green Goddess (1930). D: Alfred E. Green. C: George Arliss, Alice Joyce, H. B. Warner.

The Guilty Generation (1931). D: Rowland Lee. C: Leo Carrillo, Constance Cummings, Robert Young, Boris Karloff.

Guilty Hands (1931). D: W. S. Van Dyke. C: Lionel Barrymore, Kay Francis, Madge Evans, Alan Mowbray.

The Half-Naked Truth (1932). D: Gregory La Cava. C: Lupe Vélez, Lee Tracy, Eugene Pallette, Frank Morgan, Franklin Pangborn.

Hallelujah, I'm a Bum! (1933). D: Lewis Milestone. C: Al Jolson, Madge Evans, Frank Morgan, Harry Langdon, Chester Conklin.

Hard to Handle (1933). D: Mervyn LeRoy. C: James Cagney, Mary Brian, Ruth Donnelly, Claire Dodd, Allen Jenkins.

The Heart of New York (1932). D: Mervyn LeRoy. C: George Sidney, Joe Smith, Ruth Hall.

Heat Lightning (1934). D: Mervyn LeRoy. C: Aline MacMahon, Ann Dvorak, Preston Foster, Lyle Talbot, Glenda Farrell, Frank McHugh, Ruth Donnelly.

Hell's Highway (1932). D: Roland Brown. C: Richard Dix, Tom Brown, Charles Middleton, Clarence Muse, Rochelle Hudson.

Heroes for Sale (1933). D: William Wellman. C: Richard Barthelmess, Loretta Young, Aline MacMahon.

Hot Saturday (1932). D: William Seiter. C: Cary Grant, Nancy Carroll, Randolph Scott, Lilian Bond, Jane Darwell.

The House on 56th Street (1933). D: Robert Florey. C: Kay Francis, Margaret Lindsay, Ricardo Cortez, Gene Raymond.

I Am a Fugitive from a Chain Gang (1932). D: Mervyn LeRoy. C: Paul Muni, Glenda Farrell, Helen Vinson, Preston Foster.

If I Were Free (1933). D: Elliott Nugent. C: Irene Dunne, Clive Brook, Nils Asther.

Illicit (1931). D: Archie Mayo. C: Barbara Stanwyck, James Rennie, Ricardo Cortez, Joan Blondell.

I Sell Anything (1934). D: Robert Florey. C: Pat O'Brien, Ann Dvorak, Claire Dodd, Roscoe Karns.

Island of Lost Souls (1932). D: Erle C. Kenton. C: Charles Laughton, Bela Lugosi, Richard Arlen, Leila Hyams, Kathleen Burke.

Is My Face Red? (1932). D: William Seiter. C: Ricardo Cortez, Helen Twelvetrees, Jill Esmond.

Jewel Robbery (1932). D: William Dieterle. C: William Powell, Kay Francis, Helen Vinson, Alan Mowbray.

Jimmy the Gent (1934). D: Michael Curtiz. C: James Cagney, Bette Davis, Alice White, Mayo Methot, Allen Jenkins.

The Kennel Murder Case (1933). D: Michael Curtiz. C: William Powell, Mary Astor, Eugene Pallette.

Kept Husbands (1931). D: Lloyd Bacon. C: Dorothy Mackaill, Joel McCrea, Clara Kimball Young.

The King Murder (1932). D: Richard Thorpe. C: Conway Tearle, Natalie Moorhead.

Kongo (1932). D: William Cowen. C: Walter Huston, Lupe Vélez, Conrad Nagel, Virginia Bruce.

Ladies of Leisure (1930). D: Frank Capra. C: Barbara Stanwyck, Ralph Graves, Lowell Sherman, Marie Prevost.

Lady Killer (1933). D: Roy Del Ruth. C: James Cagney, Mae Clarke, Margaret Lindsay, Douglass Dumbrille.

The Last Flight (1931). D: William Dieterle. C: Richard Barthelmess, Johnny Mack Brown, Helen Chandler, David Manners.

Laughing Sinners (1931). D: Harry Beaumont. C: Joan Crawford, Clark Gable, Neil Hamilton, Marjorie Rambeau, Cliff Edwards, Guy Kibbee, Roscoe Karns.

Lawyer Man (1932). D: William Dieterle. C: William Powell, Joan Blondell, Claire Dodd.

Letty Lynton (1932). D: Clarence Brown. C: Joan Crawford, Robert Montgomery, Nils Asther, May Robson.

The Little Giant (1933). D: Roy Del Ruth. C: Edward G. Robinson, Mary Astor, Helen Vinson.

The Lost Patrol (1934). D: John Ford. C: Victor McLaglen, Boris Karloff, Wallace Ford, Reginald Denny, J. M. Kerrigan, Alan Hale.

The Lost Squadron (1932). D: George Archainbaud. C: Erich von Stroheim, Richard Dix, Mary Astor, Robert Armstrong, Joel McCrea.

Love Affair (1932). D: Thornton Freeland. C: Dorothy Mackaill, Humphrey Bogart.

Love Is a Racket (1932). D: William Wellman. C: Douglas Fairbanks Jr., Ann Dvorak, Frances Dee, Lee Tracy.

Madame X (1929). D: Lionel Barrymore. C: Ruth Chatterton, Lewis Stone.

The Mad Genius (1931). D: Michael Curtiz. C: John Barrymore, Marian Marsh, Charles Butterworth.

The Magician (1926). D: Rex Ingram. C: Alice Terry, Paul Wegener.

Mandalay (1934). D: Michael Curtiz. C: Kay Francis, Ricardo Cortez, Lyle Talbot, Warner Oland, Reginald Owen.

Man's Castle (1933). D: Frank Borzage. C: Spencer Tracy, Loretta Young, Marjorie Rambeau, Glenda Farrell.

The Mask of Fu Manchu (1932). D: Charles Brabin. C: Boris Karloff, Lewis Stone, Karen Morley, Myrna Loy.

Massacre (1934). D: Alan Crosland. C: Richard Barthelmess, Ann Dvorak, Dudley Digges.

Mata Hari (1931). D: George Fitzmaurice. C: Greta Garbo, Ramon Novarro, Lionel Barrymore, Lewis Stone, Karen Morley.

The Match King (1932). D: Howard Bretherton & William Keighley. C: Warren William, Lili Damita, Glenda Farrell, Claire Dodd.

The Mayor of Hell (1933). D: Archie Mayo. C: James Cagney, Madge Evans, Dudley Digges, Allen Jenkins, Frankie Darro.

Me and My Gal (1932). D: Raoul Walsh. C: Spencer Tracy, Joan Bennett, Marion Burns, J. Farrell MacDonald.

Men in White (1934). D: Richard Boleslawski. C: Clark Gable, Myrna Loy, Jean Hersholt, Otto Kruger.

Men Must Fight (1933). D: Edgar Selwyn. C: Diana Wynyard, Lewis Stone, Phillips Holmes, Hedda Hopper.

Merrily We Go to Hell (1932). D: Dorothy Arzner. C: Sylvia Sidney, Fredric March, Skeets Gallagher, Cary Grant.

Midnight Mary (1933). D: William Wellman. C: Loretta Young, Ricardo Cortez, Franchot Tone, Andy Devine, Una Merkel.

The Mind Reader (1933). D: Roy Del Ruth. C: Warren William, Constance Cummings, Allen Jenkins, Mayo Methot, Clarence Muse.

The Miracle Woman (1931). D: Frank Capra. C: Barbara Stanwyck, David Manners.

Merry Wives of Reno (1934). D: H. Bruce Humberstone. C: Guy Kibbee, Glenda Farrell, Margaret Lindsay, Hugh Herbert, Ruth Donnelly.

Morocco (1930). D: Josef von Sternberg. C: Marlene Dietrich, Gary Cooper, Adolphe Menjou.

The Most Dangerous Game (1932). D: Ernest B. Schoedsack & Irving Pichel. C: Joel McCrea, Fay Wray, Leslie Banks.

The Mummy (1932). D: Karl Freund. C: Boris Karloff, Zita Johann, David Manners, Edward Van Sloan, Noble Johnson.

Murder at the Vanities (1934). D: Mitchell Leisen. C: Carl Brisson, Victor McLaglen, Jack Oakie, Kitty Carlisle, Toby Wing, Duke Ellington Orchestra.

Murders in the Rue Morgue (1932). D: Robert Florey. C: Bela Lugosi, Sidney Fox.

Murders in the Zoo (1933). D: A. Edward Sutherland. C: Lionel Atwill, Charles Ruggles, Randolph Scott, Gail Patrick.

Mystery of the Wax Museum (1933). D: Michael Curtiz. C: Lionel Atwill, Fay Wray, Glenda Farrell, Frank McHugh.

New Morals for Old (1932). D: Charles Brabin. C: Robert Young, Margaret Perry, Lewis Stone, Laura Hope Crews.

Night Nurse (1931). D: William Wellman. C: Barbara Stanwyck, Ben Lyon, Clark Gable, Joan Blondell.

Night World (1932). D: Hobart Henley. C: Lew Ayres, Mae Clarke, Boris Karloff, Clarence Muse, Hedda Hopper, George Raft, Dorothy Revier.

Noah's Ark (1928). D: Michael Curtiz. C: Dolores Costello, George O'Brien, Noah Beery.

No More Orchids (1932). D: Walter Lang. C: Carole Lombard, Walter Connolly, Lyle Talbot.

No Other Woman (1933). D: J. Walter Ruben. C: Irene Dunne, Charles Bickford, Gwili Andre.

The Office Wife (1930). D: Lloyd Bacon. C: Dorothy Mackaill, Lewis Stone, Natalie Moorhead.

Okay America (1932). D: Tay Garnett. C: Lew Ayres, Maureen O'Sullivan, Louis Calhern, Edward Arnold.

One Way Passage (1932). D: Tay Garnett. C: William Powell, Kay Francis, Aline MacMahon, Frank McHugh

Only Yesterday (1933). D: John Stahl. C: Margaret Sullavan, John Boles, Billie Burke, Edna May Oliver.

Other Men's Women (1931). D: William Wellman. C: Grant Withers, Mary Astor, James Cagney.

Our Betters (1933). D: George Cukor. C: Constance Bennett, Gilbert Roland, Anita Louise, Violet Kemble-Cooper, Tyrell Davis.

Our Dancing Daughters (1928). D: Harry Beaumont. C: Joan Crawford, Johnny Mack Brown.

Paid (1930). D: Sam Wood. C: Joan Crawford, Douglass Montgomery, Robert Armstrong, Marie Prevost.

Parachute Jumper (1933). D: Alfred E. Green. C: Douglas Fairbanks Jr., Bette Davis, Frank McHugh.

Paris Interlude (1934). D: Edwin L. Marin. C: Robert Young, Madge Evans, Otto Kruger, Ted Healy.

Parole Girl (1933). D: Edward F. Cline. C: Mae Clarke, Ralph Bellamy, Marie Prevost.

Party Husband (1931). D: Clarence Badger. C: Dorothy Mackaill, James Rennie, Mary Doran, Donald Cook.

Penthouse (1933). D: W. S. Van Dyke. C: Warner Baxter, Myrna Loy, Mae Clarke, Phillips Holmes.

Picture Snatcher (1933). D: Lloyd Bacon. C: James Cagney, Ralph Bellamy, Alice White, Patricia Ellis.

Possessed (1931). D: Clarence Brown. C: Joan Crawford, Clark Gable, Skeets Gallagher, Wallace Ford.

The Power and the Glory (1933). D: William K. Howard. C: Spencer Tracy, Colleen Moore, Ralph Morgan, Helen Vinson.

Private Detective 62 (1933). D: Michael Curtiz. C: William Powell, Margaret Lindsay.

The Public Enemy (1931). D: William Wellman. C: James Cagney, Jean Harlow, Joan Blondell, Donald Cook, Mae Clarke.

Quick Millions (1931). D: Rowland Brown. C: Spencer Tracy, Marguerite Churchill, Sally Eilers, George Raft.

Rain (1932). D: Lewis Milestone. C: Joan Crawford, Walter Huston, William Gargan, Beulah Bondi.

The Reckless Hour (1931). D: John Francis Dillon. C: Dorothy Mackaill, Conrad Nagel, Joan Blondell.

Red Dust (1932). D: Victor Fleming. C: Clark Gable, Jean Harlow, Mary Astor, Gene Raymond, Donald Crisp, Willie Fung.

Red-Headed Woman (1932). D: Jack Conway. C: Jean Harlow, Chester Morris, Una Merkel, Leila Hyams, Lewis Stone.

Registered Nurse (1934). D: Robert Florey. C: Bebe Daniels, Lyle Talbot, John Halliday, Sidney Toler, Beulah Bondi.

Riptide (1934). D: Edmund Goulding. C: Norma Shearer, Robert Montgomery, Herbert Marshall, Mrs. Patrick Campbell, Lilyan Tashman.

The Roadhouse Murder (1932). D: J. Walter Ruben. C: Eric Linden, Dorothy Jordan, Bruce Cabot.

Road to Paradise (1930). D: William Beaudine. C: Loretta Young, Jack Mulhall.

Roar of the Dragon (1932). D: Wesley Ruggles. C: Richard Dix, Gwili Andre, Edward Everett Horton, ZaSu Pitts.

Roman Scandals (1933). D: Frank Tuttle. C: Eddie Cantor, Ruth Etting, Gloria Stuart, Edward Arnold, Verree Teasdale.

Sadie McKee (1934). D: Clarence Brown. C: Joan Crawford, Franchot Tone, Gene Raymond, Edward Arnold, Leo G. Carroll.

Safe in Hell (1931). D: William Wellman. C: Dorothy Mackaill, Donald Cook, Nina Mae McKinney, Clarence Muse.

Sailor's Luck (1933). D: Raoul Walsh. C: James Dunn, Sally Eilers, Victor Jory, Sammy Cohen.

Scarface (1932). D: Howard Hawks. C: Paul Muni, Ann Dvorak, George Raft, Karen Morley, Osgood Perkins, Boris Karloff.

Search for Beauty (1934). D: Erle C. Kenton. C: Buster Crabbe, Ida Lupino, Robert Armstrong, Toby Wing.

The Secret 6 (1931). D: George Hill. C: Wallace Beery, Lewis Stone, Clark Gable, Jean Harlow, Marjorie Rambeau, Ralph Bellamy.

Secrets of the French Police (1932). D: A. Edward Sutherland. C: Gregory Ratoff, Gwili Andre, John Warburton, Frank Morgan.

Shanghai Express (1932). D: Josef von Sternberg. C: Marlene Dietrich, Clive Brook, Anna May Wong, Warner Oland, Eugene Pallette, Gustav von Seyffertitz.

She Had to Say Yes (1933). D: Busby Berkeley & George Amy. Loretta Young, Lyle Talbot, Winnie Lightner, Regis Toomey.

Shopworn (1932). D: Nick Grinde. C: Barbara Stanwyck, Regis Toomey, ZaSu Pitts, Clara Blandick.

Show Girl in Hollywood (1930). D: Mervyn LeRoy. C: Alice White, Jack Mulhall, Blanche Sweet.

Side Show (1931). D: Roy Del Ruth. C: Winnie Lightner, Charles Butterworth, Evalyn Knapp.

The Sign of the Cross (1932). D: Cecil B. DeMille. C: Fredric March, Claudette Colbert, Elissa Landi, Charles Laughton.

The Sin of Madelon Claudet (1931). D: Edgar Selwyn. C: Helen Hayes, Lewis Stone, Neil Hamilton.

The Sin of Nora Moran (1933). D: Phil Goldstone. C: Zita Johann, Alan Dinehart, John Miljan, Paul Cavanagh.

Skyscraper Souls (1932). D: Edgar Selwyn. C: Warren William, Maureen O'Sullivan, Anita Page, Verree Teasdale, Gregory Ratoff, Wallace Ford, Hedda Hopper.

Smarty (1934). D: Robert Florey. C: Joan Blondell, Warren William, Edward Everett Horton, Claire Dodd, Frank McHugh.

The Squaw Man (1931). D: Cecil B. DeMille. C: Warner Baxter, Lupe Vélez.

The Star Witness (1931). D: William Wellman. C: Walter Huston, Sally Blane, Chic Sale.

Storm at Daybreak (1933). D: Richard Boleslawski. C: Kay Francis, Walter Huston, Nils Asther.

The Story of Temple Drake (1933). D: Stephen Roberts. C: Miriam Hopkins, William Gargan, Jack La Rue, Florence Eldridge, Irving Pichel.

The Strange Love of Molly Louvain (1932). D: Michael Curtiz. C: Ann Dvorak, Lee Tracy.

Strangers May Kiss (1931). D: George Fitzmaurice. C: Norma Shearer, Robert Montgomery, Neil Hamilton.

Street of Women (1932). D: Archie Mayo. C: Kay Francis, Roland Young, Alan Dinehart, Gloria Stuart.

Street Scene (1931). D: King Vidor. C: Sylvia Sidney, William Collier Jr., Estelle Taylor, Beulah Bondi, David Landau.

Supernatural (1933). D: Victor Halperin. C: Carole Lombard, Randolph Scott, Alan Dinehart, Vivienne Osborne.

Susan Lenox (Her Fall and Rise) (1931). D: Robert Z. Leonard. C: Greta Garbo, Clark Gable, Jean Hersholt, Alan Hale.

Symphony of Six Million (1932). D: Gregory La Cava. C: Irene Dunne, Ricardo Cortez, Gregory Ratoff.

Tarzan and His Mate (1934). D: Cedric Gibbons. C: Johnny Weissmuller, Maureen O'Sullivan.

Taxi (1932). D: Roy Del Ruth. C: James Cagney, Loretta Young, George E. Stone, Guy Kibbee.

They Had to See Paris (1929). D: Frank Borzage. C: Will Rogers, Irene Rich.

Thirteen Women (1932). D: George Archainbaud. C: Irene Dunne, Myrna Loy, Ricardo Cortez, Jill Esmond.

This Day and Age (1933). D: Cecil B. DeMille. C: Charles Bickford, Judith Allen, Richard Cromwell, Bradley Page.

Three on a Match (1932). D: Mervyn LeRoy. C: Warren William, Joan Blondell, Bette Davis, Ann Dvorak, Lyle Talbot, Humphrey Bogart.

Three Wise Girls (1932). D: William Beaudine. C: Jean Harlow, Mae Clarke, Marie Prevost.

Tide of Empire (1929). D: Allan Dwan. C: Renée Adorée, Tom Keene.

Torch Singer (1933). D: Alexander Hall & George Somnes. C: Claudette Colbert, Ricardo Cortez, David Manners.

Turn Back the Clock (1933). D: Edgar Selwyn. C: Lee Tracy, Mae Clarke, Otto Kruger.

20,000 Years in Sing Sing (1932). D: Michael Curtiz. C: Spencer Tracy, Bette Davis, Lyle Talbot, Louis Calhern, Warren Hymer.

Two Seconds (1932). D: Mervyn LeRoy. C: Edward G. Robinson, Vivienne Osborne, Preston Foster, Guy Kibbee, J. Carrol Naish.

Under Eighteen (1931). D: Archie Mayo. C: Marian Marsh, Regis Toomey, Warren William, Anita Page.

Union Depot (1932). D: Alfred E Green. C: Douglas Fairbanks Jr., Joan Blondell, Guy Kibbee, Alan Hale, David Landau.

Upperworld (1934). D: Roy Del Ruth. C: Warren William, Mary Astor, Ginger Rogers, Andy Devine, Dickie Moore.

Virtue (1932). D: Edward Buzzell. C: Carole Lombard, Pat O'Brien, Ward Bond, Mayo Methot, Jack La Rue.

The Voice of the City (1929). D: Willard Mack. C: Willard Mack, Robert Ames, Sylvia Field.

War Nurse (1930). D: Edgar Selwyn. C: Robert Montgomery, June Walker, Anita Page, Marie Prevost.

Washington Merry-Go-Round (1932). D: James Cruze. C: Lee Tracy, Constance Cummings, Walter Connolly.

Waterloo Bridge (1931). D: James Whale. C: Mae Clarke, Douglass Montgomery.

Week-End Marriage (1932). D: Thornton Freeland. C: Loretta Young, Norman Foster, Aline MacMahon.

West of the Divide (1934). D: Robert N. Bradbury. C: John Wayne, Gabby Hayes, Yakima Canutt.

When Ladies Meet (1933). D: Harry Beaumont. C: Ann Harding, Robert Montgomery, Myrna Loy.

White Woman (1933). D: Stuart Walker. C: Charles Laughton, Carole Lombard, Charles Bickford.

White Zombie (1932). D: Victor Halperin. C: Bela Lugosi, Madge Bellamy.

Wild Boys of the Road (1933). D: William Wellman. C: Frankie Darro, Rochelle Hudson, Sterling Holloway.

The Witching Hour (1934). D: Henry Hathaway. C: Sir Guy Standing, John Halliday.

The Woman Racket (1930). D: Albert Kelley & Robert Ober. C: Tom Moore, Blanche Sweet.

Wonder Bar (1934). D: Lloyd Bacon. C: Al Jolson, Kay Francis, Dolores del Rio, Ricardo Cortez, Dick Powell, Ruth Donnelly, Fifi D'Orsay.

Geoffrey O'Brien is the author of nine collections of poetry, including most recently *The Blue Hill*, winner of the Marsh Hawk Poetry Prize for 2017, and *Who Goes There* (2020). He has published eleven prose books encompassing memoir, cultural history, and criticism, among them *Hardboiled America* (1981), *Dream Time: Chapters from the Sixties* (1988), *The Phantom Empire* (1993), *Bardic Deadlines: Reviewing Poetry, 1984-95* (1998), *The Browser's Ecstasy* (2000), *Sonata for Jukebox* (2004), *The Fall of the House of Walworth* (2010), *Stolen Glimpses, Captive Shadows: Writing on Film 2002-2012* (2013), and *Where Did Poetry Come From: Some Early Encounters* (2020). He was editor-in-chief of Library of America from 1998 to 2017 and has contributed frequently to *The New York Review of Books*, *Film Comment*, *Artforum*, and other periodicals.